ANGELINE'S GIFT

JESSICA SAMUELS

Copyright © 2025 by Jessica Samuels

All rights reserved.

No part of this book may be reproduced in any form or by any electronic or mechanical means, including information storage and retrieval systems, without written permission from the author, except for the use of brief quotations in a book review.

This is a work of fiction!

❧ Created with Vellum

To the family and friends that have been there from the beginning!

Chapter One
ANGELINE'S BIRTH

Angeline was born on the coldest day of the century. They were having a record-breaking snow fall and her parents were stuck in a snow drift after trying to get to the hospital. There wasn't anyone around and they were alone while Estelle pushed as hard as she could to get Angeline into the world.

This story had been told every year since Angeline was born, and now she was turning thirty. Her parents sat her down at the kitchen table that was laid out with all of her favorite foods. Angeline looked over the dinner and raised her eyebrows at her mother.

"This is all very nice mom, but why did you go through all of this trouble for three people?" Angeline asked.

"We have something to discuss with you." Estelle said, with a worried look on her face.

Michael was sitting at the head of the table with the same worried expression on his face.

"Dad? What's with the look?" Angeline asked.

"Let's eat before this gets cold." Michael said.

"Okay." Angeline said.

Angeline could tell there was something important going on even if they didn't tell her right away. She let her mind wonder, and settled on the prospect of a gift. It was a car or something and they were having a hard time keeping it a secret.

Estelle took her seat and started passing each dish to Angeline and then over to Michael. When everyone had what they wanted the intense silence was more than she could handle.

"This is really good, but with all the silence it feels more like a funeral than a birthday party." Angeline said.

Estelle sighed and looked over at Michael. Michael closed his eyes and gave her a slight nod. Angeline waited for everything to come out.

"On the night of your birth everything was covered in white. The temperature was well below freezing and we got stuck in a snowbank…

"Oh, the birth story in the middle of dinner." Angeline said.

"This is important Angeline." Michael chastised her.

"I've heard it every year for thirty years now. I can't see why it's important when I can recite it word for word." Angeline said.

"It's important because you don't know everything." Michael said.

"Okay, let's hear the story. Start to finish the whole story." Angeline said.

Estelle cleared her throat and looked at her daughter.

"On the night you were born we were trying to get to the hospital and crashed the car into a snowbank. There's no way anyone could see the car from the road, or even detect how many people were in it." Estelle said, pausing for a moment.

Angeline took a bite of her chicken, bacon, ranch pasta and chewed slowly. Estelle seeing that she had her daughter's full attention took a steadying breath.

"Our car was covered by the snow, and I was doing everything I could to pant through the contractions. Angeline you were determined to be born right there in that car no matter how stuck we were." Estelle said.

"Sounds like me, determined, stubborn, and right now." Angeline joked.

"You were indeed." Michael said smiling.

"Okay, how did you get out of the snowbank? I don't think you ever told me that part." Angeline asked.

Estelle looked at Michael and then back at Angeline.

"We saw a light through the snow and were thankful someone rescued us. Only the light was from an amulet worn by the woman who found us.

We're not sure if she was on the road when we crashed, or if she saw our taillights. Either way she found us in that snowbank. Her amulet shone brighter then anything I'd ever seen. Her name was Gaia, and you're wearing that amulet now. She gave it to you as a gift after she helped deliver you and then helped us get to the hospital. She whispered something in your ear and then kissed your forehead. After that she visited us in the hospital one more time before we were released." Estelle said smiling.

"I've worn this necklace on my birthday every year, and usually it's accompanied by earrings and a ring that kind of match." Angeline said.

"That amulet will protect you through anything and everything. Gaia said that on your thirtieth birthday you'd start to understand the meaning of that amulet. Have you noticed anything different?" Estelle asked.

Angeline looked at the amulet and then up at her mother.

"Nothing out of the ordinary. It stays unusually cold all the time." Angeline replied.

"It never warms against your skin?" Michael asked.

"Not like a normal necklace would. It's cold to the touch." Angeline replied.

Estelle looked at Michael and he gave her a worried look back.

"Why are you two so secretive? You're acting like

I'm going to parish in front of you or something." Angeline said.

"When you were finally born you weren't breathing. As a matter of fact, your skin was completely blue, and Gaia breathed your first breath for you. I'd always hoped she would return, but she never has. I guess that's why I was hoping that even now on this day she'd come around." Estelle said.

"I never knew that part of the story either. Why did you keep this part from me all this time?" Angeline asked.

"Because we were scared. We're even more worried now that you've turned thirty." Estelle replied.

"I'd be happy to talk to her if she ever comes around." Angeline said.

"If she does tell her to visit us. We'd like to thank her for everything she did with your birth." Estelle said.

Michael seemed to relax and started eating his dinner. Angeline picked up her fork and took a bite of her pasta. Michael choosing fried chicken ate with a new-found vigor until his plate was cleaned.

When the ice cream cake came out of the freezer a knock sounded on the door…

Chapter Two
FELIX'S BEGINNING

Felix zoomed down the interstate with his music up as loud as it could go and the top down. The weather was warm on the island and the palm trees were swaying in the wind. The closer he got to the largest mountain on the island he started to feel hotter.

His phone rang and Felix pulled off the road to a small taco stand. He fumbled for a minute before he found his phone in the console and picked it up. He smiled and answered it.

"Hello Ma, how's it going?" Felix said cheerfully.

"I'm good son, but why are you out there by that old volcano?" His mother asked.

"You're better than a PI, how did you know I was out here?" Felix asked.

"Hello, my name is Natalia Costas your mother, and better than any FBI agent out there when it comes to locating her only child." His mother replied.

"Of course, but you're using the crystal ball." Felix said joking.

"Well. That still doesn't answer why you're out there at that old volcano." Natalia said.

"I don't know why I'm here. I felt drawn to this place for some reason." Felix replied.

"I guess now is better than never." Natalia said.

"Okay, why don't you explain that statement." Felix said.

"You've never asked, and we've never divulged, so bear with me while we go through this." Natalia said.

"Go through what exactly?" Felix asked.

"I hope you're pulled over son." Natalia said.

"I'm good, I'm on the side of the road." Felix replied.

"You were born on the side of that mountain road. Your father and I were on our way to a resort near to mile marker twenty-three." Natalia started.

"I'm pulled off on that mile marker now." Felix said shocked.

"Is that little store still sitting there? It was old back then and looked like it was falling, so I doubt it's still there." Natalia said.

Felix took a quick picture and sent it to Natalia.

"I just sent you a picture of what's here. You tell me if it's the same place." Felix said.

Natalia takes a minute and looks at the picture.

"That's the place. I can't believe it's still standing." Natalia said.

"That's where I'm at now. What does this place have to do with anything?" Felix asked.

"You were born in that parking lot area. It was dark that night and the volcano was at the top of that mountain. I went into labor, and you were coming fast, and about five weeks early. That's when we saw the lava at the top of the volcano start to spark. It was like huge blobs just popping up, but it didn't ever spill out. We were watching it and trying to get turned around to go back down the mountain, but there wasn't any time." Natalia said.

"Maybe that's why I'm drawn to this area then." Felix said.

"Maybe, or maybe it was the man who showed up out of nowhere." Natalia said.

"What man?" Felix asked.

"I'm not sure to this day who he was, but your father was standing outside of the car. He had just helped me get into a laying down position in the back of the car and tapped your father on the shoulder. Your father was startled, but the man said he was a doctor and asked if he could help assist. I said yes immediately so thankful that a doctor was there. Then he just disappeared as fast as he appeared." Natalia said.

"Was he just out for a stroll while the volcano was erupting?" Felix asked.

"The volcano never erupted. You can look in all the papers at the time of your birth and there's nothing about the volcano erupting. There's not even anything about the doctor who helped deliver you. He just appeared out of nowhere, and as soon as you were born he whispered something in your ear and handed you over. He said he would visit again in thirty years and walked away. He went into the darkness and wasn't ever seen again from my understanding." Natalia said.

"Did you not watch for him?" Felix asked.

"No, we were too busy looking at you and trying to get back to the city. We had to get you somewhere safe and check out fast. You were born early, and on the side of a mountain." Natalia explained.

"Did you ask anyone about the volcano eruption?" Felix asked.

"Yes, we went to the small town at the base of the mountain, and they said that volcano hadn't erupted in over a thousand years." Natalia replied.

"There's a village up this road about three miles from where I'm at. Did you ever check there?" Felix asked.

"No, I didn't know there was a village up there." Natalia replied.

"Where's Dad? He has to know where that lodge was he was taking you to." Felix said.

"I'm here son, but the resort we were going to isn't far from where you're at. If you take that road in front of the store up the mountain about two miles you'll find the resort we were going to. It's a small place with a few cabins on a hiking trail." Frank explained.

"Frank tell him about the lake up there." Natalia urged.

"There's a lake up there that stays hot no matter what the temperature is. It's not as hot as a geyser but it's not as cool as the hot springs. I think they've reported deaths from it, but I'm not sure." Frank replied.

"Is the lake close to the resort?" Felix asked.

"We never made it up there to see. When we decided to go to the resort it was based off what a friend of mine told me. I thought it sounded interesting, but then you decided to be born." Frank replied chuckling.

"You're funny dad, but I think I'm going to go check it out. You've never told me about any of this and knowing what it's all about now I'm ready to see what it's like." Felix said.

"Alright, take pictures I'd like to see what it looks like." Frank said.

"Why don't you meet me out here and we can go together." Felix asked.

"Alright, sit and wait we can be there in a half an hour." Frank replied.

"Sounds good, I'm going into this little general store and getting some supplies. We can finally rent one of those cabins." Felix said.

"I'll gather some things from here too. We might not get to stay, but we can have a nice meal just the same." Natalia said.

Felix agreed and went into the small general store.

He pushed his sunglasses to the top of his head and looked around. There was a man sitting at the counter reading a newspaper.

"Welcome to The General Store." The man said.

"Hi, is the name of the place The General Store?" Felix asked.

"Yes." The man said, his eyes never leaving the newspaper.

"How long has this store been here?" Felix asked.

"Oh, I don't know. I'd say well over a hundred years." The man replied.

"Wow! I'm surprised it lasted this long." Felix said.

"This old building has a few hundred years left in her. My ancestors built it with their bare hands." The man said.

"That's the best kind of craftsmanship." Felix said.

"Yes, it is is there something special you're looking for here?" The man asked.

"Just some snacks, and drinks. I'm looking for a cabin, or a resort that's around here. Do you know where that might be?" Felix asked.

"There's a few cabins up around the bend that are rented out from time to time, but this wouldn't be a good season for that." The man replied.

"Why not?" Felix asked.

"Lava Rock Lake that's up there, is too hot right now. The volcano is threatening to erupt again, but I don't see it happening." The man replied.

"Does it erupt often?" Felix asked.

"No." The man replied.

"When was the last time it erupted?" Felix asked.

"It goes through a cycle about every thirty years or so. It'll spew out some junk that clouds the skies, and then it'll just settle down. I've never known it to actually flow, but the village at the base of the actual volcano says it flows freely. Ah, they've got their own legends up there." The man replied.

"Would they know the legends of the child that was born in this parking lot thirty years ago today?" Felix asked.

"The one the mysterious man helped deliver?" The man asked.

"Yes, I believe the mysterious man was a doctor." Felix replied.

"I've heard him called many things, but never a doctor." The man said.

"Oh, is he not a doctor?" Felix asked.

"Why are you so interested in this story son?" The man asked.

"I was the child born in this parking lot thirty years ago." Felix replied.

The man narrowed his eyes at Felix and looked him over. He then reached down slowly, and Felix tensed hoping the man wasn't grabbing a gun. Reflectively Felix held up his hands and took a step back.

The man opened a drawer slowly and pulled out a note and sat it on the counter. Felix watched him with an intensity that was written all over his face.

"Calm down son. Your parents left this note on my door that night." The man said.

Felix lowered his hands slowly and looked at the note. It looked like his father's handwriting, but he wasn't sure. Felix picked up the worn paper and started reading it.

"To whom it may concern,

I'm truly sorry for the mess left in the parking lot. My wife went into labor, and we had no choice but to deliver the baby with the aid of the doctor. We will return to pay for the damage.

Regards.

Frank Blazer

"That would be my father." Felix said setting the note back down on the counter.

"I was given ten thousand dollars a year after that." The man replied.

"Really?" Felix asked surprised.

"Yes, it was delivered by a courier every year on this day since then." The man replied.

"Have you received it this year?" Felix asked.

"Yes, it was delivered this morning." The man replied.

"My parents didn't tell me about that." Felix said.

The man just nodded his head and gave him a tight smile. Felix paid for his purchase and stepped back out into the warm air. He looked around and saw the sky had darkened a little, but didn't think much of it. It was normal in this area for the weather to change unexpectedly.

Felix waited beside his car and watched the sky darken. When stuff started falling from the sky Felix reached out and touched it. He rubbed his fingers together and noticed it was ash.

Looking up at the mountain in front of him he knew immediately it was the volcano. It was threatening to erupt and Felix wanted to go watch it. His parents showed up as the ash started to settle on everything.

CHAPTER THREE

Angeline

After dinner Angeline sat and thought about the information her parents gave her. Her birth was traumatic, but a stranger helped her mother. This all seemed to be some kind of fever dream they had. In the last thirty years Angeline has never heard of anything so dramatic.

After they'd rested for a while and enjoyed the day Angeline bid her parents farewell. She was driving towards the city when the snow started to fall. It had been many years since the snow had fallen on her birthday and she took the opportunity to play for a bit.

Angeline pulled over on the side of the road in a clearing and got out of her car. She stepped to the middle of the old country road and tilted her face up to the sky. Angeline could feel every snowflake that touched her face, and allowed it to cool her skin.

Angeline stood there letting the snow cover her for a long time. When she finally opened her eyes again she saw a woman walking towards her. The woman smiled as she approached in her heavy cloak that shielded her face.

"It's a lovely day isn't it?" The woman asked.

"It's a perfect day." Angeline replied.

"I'm inclined to agree. Tell me girl, why are you standing in the middle of this road at such a sight as this?" The woman asked.

"I'm not sure. I was driving by and felt drawn to it, so I stopped and took a moment to enjoy the snow." Angeline replied.

"I visit this spot every year hoping a young woman would stop here. She's a very special woman, and this spot means a great deal to her life." The woman said looking around.

"This spot is very important to my beginning in this life." Angeline said.

The woman looked at Angeline intently squinting her eyes to looking deep into Angelin's soul.

"Are you Angeline Mistique?" The woman asked.

"Who did you say you were again?" Angeline asked.

"You are indeed. You were born here on the side of the road where your car sits. I was there that night." The woman said.

"How...

"I never forget the beautiful children I've gifted in this life. You're thirty years old today. Tell me, did your parents tell you about me?" The woman asked.

"Yes, but they didn't tell me your name." Angeline replied skeptically.

"I guess we didn't have enough time for pleasantries at the time of your birth." The woman said.

"No, I would assume you didn't." Angeline said keeping her eyes trained on the amulet the woman wore around her neck.

"I can see you're drawn to this old thing." The woman said.

"It glows does it not?" Angeline asked.

"Yes, but only if I need it to." The woman replied.

"It's odd, I feel like I've known you forever and I still don't know your name." Angeline said.

"I'm Hecate." She said and bowed her head for a moment.

"Why does that sound familiar?" Angeline asked more to herself than to Hecate.

"I'm not sure child, why do you assume you'd know the name?" Hecate asked.

"You've got the same name as the Greek Goddess in Greek Mythology. I knew I'd heard it somewhere just couldn't place it. Sorry about that, sometimes I have to give things a true thought to bring it into fruition." Angeline replied.

"So, you've heard of me, but do you know the whole truth about me?" Hecate asked.

"I studied Greek Mythology in college, but it was

as pastime kind of thing to get through. I know that you're the goddess of craft, and I assume you're the only one of your kind." Angeline replied.

"I am indeed the goddess of craft, but it's witchcraft. Do you know anything about that?" Hecate asked.

"Like tarot cards and stuff?" Angeline asked.

"That's part of it, but not all of it." Hecate replied.

"Okay, so did you bring on this snowstorm?" Angeline asked bluntly.

"No, it would be nice, but no matter how hard I try I can't control the weather. There's only one God who can do that, and I've never met Him." Hecate replied.

"You believe in God?" Angeline asked raising an eyebrow.

"Yes, of course I do. He's the most powerful God out there. I mean there's Zeus, but he's part of my world now isn't he." Hecate replied.

"Yes, but knowing all of this just brings up so many questions." Angeline said.

"I can imagine, but what I'm shocked about is that you're so willing to believe me." Hecate said.

"I believe in taking people at face value." Angeline said.

"Very good, do you know about your gift?" Hecate asked.

"What gift?" Angeline asked.

"I told you that I remember every child I give a

gift to, and you're one of those children." Hecate replied holding out her hand.

Angeline took Hecate's hand and felt a jolt of lightning pulse through her. She didn't know what was happening when the flashing started in front of her. Angeline couldn't see Hecate standing in front of her because of the flashing.

It seemed like it was taking forever for the flashing to stop. When it did Angeline collapsed to the ground. Hecate bent over Angeline's unresponsive body and touched her forehead.

When the ground started to shake Hecate turned and walked away leaving Angeline on the cold wet ground. The snow started to fall faster and soon Angeline's body was covered.

CHAPTER FOUR

Felix stood next to his parents at the edge of the village. He'd never seen a village like this before. Everything was very ancient, and untouched by the outside world.

A man walked up to the trio and gave them a toothless smile. Frank smiled back at the man and gave him a polite nod. Natalia and Felix gave him a polite nod and waited for Frank to do the talking.

"Are you here to watch the eruption of the volcano?" The older man asked.

"Does it ever actually erupt?" Frank asked.

"That volcano erupts every thirty years for three days." The old man said.

"Why every thirty years for three days?" Felix asked.

"Ah, the males are born, and their fates are sealed. You boy are the product of that thirty years and three days." The old man replied.

"How do you know that?" Natalia asked his voice a hoarse whisper.

"I was there the day he was born. Our true leader came from the center of the earth to visit as he does every thirty years. We saw you as you pulled into the store as the volcano erupted." The old man replied.

"The people down in the town said the volcano hasn't erupted in centuries." Frank said.

"The volcano does erupt, but what's born of the volcano isn't lava." The old man said.

"So, what is it?" Felix asked.

"Come, I'll let him explain." The old man replied waving his hand for them to follow.

The three of them followed the older man to the end of the village. There was a small bungalow house that looked like it was made of mud, and the roof was a typical leaf type roof that was seen all around the village. The older man rang the bell that was hanging on the outside of the entrance and then got on his hands and knees to bow.

Felix eyed the man and knew exactly who he was. Frank and Natalia narrowed their eyes in recognition, but couldn't quite place him. The three of them bowed their heads slightly their eyes never leaving this man's face.

"Hello Maurice, please stand up." The man said.

"Thank you, Lord Pan I'd like to introduce you..."

"Thank you Maurice, I've been expecting them." Lord Pan said.

Felix's head snapped up and he eyed Lord Pan.

"Lord Pan? The God of the wild earth?" Felix asked.

"I see you've heard of me." Lord Pan replied.

"I've done extensive studies about you and your work." Felix said.

"Good, then you know what you are." Lord Pan said.

"What do you mean, what I am?" Felix asked.

"Does that volcano draw you to it?" Lord Pan asked.

Felix turned his attention to the volcano behind the small bungalow. It did draw him, and he could feel his body heat up from the inside. The intensity of it shimmered all over his body in a kaleidoscope of colors.

Natalia shrieked in surprise as the light surrounding Felix intensified. Frank took a step back pulling Natalia with him. Felix turned and looked Lord Pan who crossed his arms in pride.

"What's happening to me?" Felix asked.

"You're in your true form now Felix." Lord Pan replied.

Felix caught a glimpse of his shadow when he turned to look at the fear on his parents faces. He stopped and looked at the shadow confused at what he was looking at. He blinked several times, trying to grasp what he was.

The shadow was larger than anything Felix had ever seen. It was tall and it wide, but when he felt his body it was normal. Felix turned to

Lord Pan and his eyes started to glow a deep fiery red.

"How do you feel?" Lord Pan asked.

"Alive." Felix replied.

"Good, you've come into your true form Felix." Lord Pan said.

"Why does my true form look like a dragon?" Felix asked.

Lord Pan turned to Frank who was rubbing his hands together.

"This is your father he was born thirty years before you were, right here in this village." Lord Pan said.

"Does everyone see me as this form when I'm in it?" Felix asked.

"No, your outer appearance will stay the same as it has always been. Only when the call comes will you turn into this true form. Your shadow will reflect your form, but only to the ones who are your target." Lord Pan replied.

"Am I a dragon?" Felix asked.

"Yes, and you'll come into all of your power within the next few years. It could take up to five, but this is the time when you learn everything you can about who you are. When the time is right you'll meet someone very important and that someone will teach you the rest of what you are." Lord pan explained.

"Does this person know they're supposed to be teaching me?" Felix asked.

"No, when you meet the person you'll know it." Lord Pan replied.

"Will they know it?" Felix asked.

"Yes, together the two of you will learn to control, life, and how to conquer the world you live in." Lord Pan replied.

"Son, this person will be your mate." Natalia said.

"I have a mate?" Felix asked.

"Yes, just like I did." Frank replied.

"Mom, why did you look so surprised when you saw me transform?" Felix asked.

"Because I've never seen it before. Your father's first time transforming was a ritual, but since you didn't make it to the village I didn't get to plan it." Natalia replied.

"I don't understand." Felix said.

"This is the most important transition of your life. You learn the human ways for the first thirty years of your life and then you learn your immortality after that. Once you transform the first time it comes natural to you. You however have a very different look than what I'm accustomed to." Natalia said.

"Why does that surprise you?" Felix asked.

"The aura of each creature and human are very interchangeable. You possess the colors like a kaleidoscope. That's never been seen before. The way your true form shimmers is like you radiate with a magic that I can't place." Natalia replied.

"Because of his mate." Lord Pan said.

"What?" Natalia asked.

"His power is fed off his mate and his shifting will happen once he's met her. Her power is mighty, and she is why you can't recognize his magic." Lord Pan replied.

"Does she have me blocked?" Natalia asked.

"She's powerful, and chosen. You'll do well to treat her with respect." Lord Pan replied.

"I treat everyone with respect." Natalia said.

Lord Pan touched the side of his nose with his right finger and Natalia's mouth set in a grim line. She didn't know what Lord Pan knew, but she hadn't always been as kind to people as she should have been.

"I know what you're thinking Natalia, and yes you've met his mate in passing and you were rude to her. Be prepared for her to recognize you." Lord Pan said interrupting her thoughts.

"My apologies my Lord, but how was I to know?" Natalia asked.

"The first rule of this gracious gift is to embrace the ones who are weaker than you are and secure their safety. You being rude is beneath you." Lord Pan replied.

"I understand and accept the punishment that I've warranted." Natalia said.

"Your punishment isn't in my hands ma'am." Lord Pan said.

"Do I need to reach out to Hecate?" Natalia asked.

"You can try, but she doesn't assign the punishment either." Lord Pan replied.

"How do I atone for this?" Natalia asked.

"You'll find out when the time is right." Lord Pan replied.

Natalia knew what that meant and now she would have be on her best behavior. This punishment would come when she least expected it and she needed to be prepared. Natalia let out a breath and looked to Frank for help.

Frank clasped his hand around Natalia's and gave her a reassuring squeeze. Felix allowed himself to calm down and his true form shadow shifted back into the human form he recognized. He could still feel the volcano pulling him, but he had to learn how to control this urge to leap.

CHAPTER FIVE

Angeline

Angeline woke up covered in snow, but she wasn't cold. She felt like she was alive for the first time in a long time. She walked back to her car and got in.

Looking out over the horizon she saw the snow had fallen more than she'd ever seen. Angeline pulled away from the side of the road and headed towards the city. She couldn't keep her mind off Hecate and what she'd said.

Angeline felt a surge of adrenaline flow through her, and she pressed her foot down on the gas. She was back in the city in half the time it would normally take. Slowing down when she got into the city limits Angeline drove through until she got to the other side.

Blinking and looking around at the area Angeline didn't know where she was. In the distance she saw a very large building that looked like a compound. She was being drawn to this place, but didn't know it even existed.

The closer Angeline got to the well-lit building she finally saw a sign. She read it aloud to herself in the car.

"NEXT STAR REHABILITATION."

Angeline had no idea what Next Star was, or why she was drawn there. Taking a right turn just past the sign she found herself driving up to what she can now see as many buildings as possible that were no more than seven stories high. She pulled into a parking spot and got out of her car.

Looking around at the buildings she could see faces looking back at her. This sparked her curiosity wondering if it was a hospital of sorts. Before Angeline could go into the building Hecate appeared before her.

"Ah, ah, you need to be dressed appropriately to go inside there." Hecate said.

Startled Angeline looked at Hecate confused.

"What's wrong with my clothes?" Angeline asked.

"You're soaked to the bone. If you want to go inside there then you need to be prepared." Hecate replied.

"What is this place?" Angeline asked.

"This is Next Star Rehab; it's a place where they bring people who may or may not have certain kinds of abilities." Hecate replied.

"Are they experimenting on people in there?" Angeline asked.

"Yes, and you're going undercover." Hecate replied.

"You've told me that I'm a born witch of sorts, and you want me to go inside this place and get captured?" Angeline asked.

"No, I want you to go inside and gather intel as a nurse. You're applying for a job in there. I'm looking for someone who was born around the same time you were, and she's trapped in this place." Hecate replied.

"I can see all of those people looking at me." Angeline said.

"You're seeing ghost from the past and present. If you come across the dead you'll need to cross them over before you can gain access to the living." Hecate said.

"Why?" Angeline asked.

"Because they won't allow you entry if you don't. The leaders of this place have been trying to get rid of them for a long time, so don't get rid of all of them." Hecate replied.

"How will I know the difference between the living and the dead?" Angeline asked.

"Trust your gut. You'll know right away who is living and who isn't." Hecate replied.

"Why haven't you ended this place already? You're powerful, and can obviously appear where you want to." Angeline asked.

"This place is warded against me. It's ran by a very powerful being who's using stolen magic to keep me out. You're powerful on your own without coming into your power, so you can get in and do what's needed to shut him down." Hecate replied.

"Who is he?" Angeline asked.

"You'll see when you're safely inside. Any knowledge of him prior to your entrance can cause an uproar and you'll be captured. I need you to be smart about this." Hecate replied.

"I can do that, but shouldn't I wait until daylight to go inside?" Angeline asked.

"No, they don't get started until the sun sets. The daytime hours are for sleeping. People who usually go in do not come back out Angeline. I need you to come back out." Hecate replied.

"I'll be able to leave at the end of my shift won't I?" Angeline asked.

"If you're able to play the game then yes. If you don't do the right thing then you'll be caught and become an experiment." Hecate replied.

"You've said that twice now, and now I'm scared." Angeline said.

"No need to be scared, just make sure you're on point." Hecate replied.

"I feel a strong presence pulling me towards that mountain over there." Angeline said.

"That would be your mate. When the time is right you'll meet your mate and when that time comes this order will be completed." Hecate said.

"I have a mate?" Angeline asked.

"Yes, and he's got power as you do, but he will feed off your power and you will feed off his. It's like a transfer of power to the person who needs it the most at the moment. Just be careful or else he can drain you." Hecate replied.

"I have no desire to be mated." Angeline said.

"When you meet him you won't be able to resist. Your heart is connected to him already." Hecate said.

"Why? Shouldn't I have a choice of who my mate is?" Angeline asked.

"You're mated at conception, and that's something that is a birthright. When you see him you'll understand." Hecate replied.

"I'll trust the process, but I'm not happy about it. For now, I want to know more ab out this place." Angeline asked waving her hand towards the buildings.

"This place is invisible to anyone who isn't gifted. Once you've come into your gift then you're able to see this place and become part of it. If you choose to become part of it then you're choosing to accept the good and the bad. The bad that happens here is beyond anything you've ever seen." Hecate said.

"Why?" Angeline asked.

"Why what?" Hecate asked.

"All of it. Why is it only visible if you're not fully human? Why is there good and bad in this place?" Angeline asked.

"This entire building is an illusion to humans. I know of one time that a human saw this place and went stark raving mad. After that Sage, the owner and operator of this place put the spell around it to make it invisible to humans. Incidentally, that's also the spell to cast me out." Hecate replied.

"Are you and this Sage person enemies?" Hecate asked.

"Yes and no. Sage was gifted at the time of his birth from Lord Pan. Only Lord Pan can gift males. We as a whole agreed on this. We knew from the time that Sage was born that he wasn't who he was born to be. His mate was also a male, and when they met they fell in love. Sage was tapped in a body that didn't conform to his truth, and he underwent a human change to make him into a female. We agreed from the beginning that he wasn't a male, but we wanted him to be transformed with magic instead of human ways. Sage didn't want to wait for the magic to take hold and now he's depressed. Because of this his transformation was botched. I can fix it, but he doesn't want me to." Hecate explained.

"If Sage was transitioning from male to female then why do you still call them a he?" Angeline asked.

"Sage requested it. He said that since his surgery was botched, and he wasn't able to fully transition then he had to stay the male he was born as." Hecate replied.

"What's the difference in his transition in the human realm and what you can do?" Angeline asked.

"If I had transitioned him with magic then he would have been a woman in every way. His body, mind, soul, and heart would have been transitioned. He asked that he be transitioned on the spot, but it takes time to rebuild a person from the inside out and he didn't want to wait. He would have also had to give up his gift and he didn't want that. He wanted both gifts within himself and that's not something that we could allow. That much power in one being is too much." Hecate explained.

"Is that why he built this place?" Angeline asked.

"Yes, he built it to draw in creatures and supernatural beings. He wanted to experiment on them and see what it was that made them who they are." Hecate replied.

"What kind of creatures does he have locked up in there?" Angelie asked looking at one of the windows that caught her eye.

"There's beings out there that aren't what you would call real, but they are. At different times in life, they've become these things, and we've accepted them." Hecate replied.

"Such as?" Angeline asked.

"Vampires, witches, dragons, ghost, werewolves, shapeshifters, and who knows what else." Hecate replied.

"I feel like there's celestial beings inside that building." Angeline said.

"I'm sure you do, which is why you've got to take on this task." Hecate replied.

"Can I help Sage transition while I'm in there without them knowing what I'm doing?" Angeline asked.

"They'd like that, but you have to be very careful

doing something like that. If he figures out what's happening then he'll turn on you." Hecate replied.

"How do we change his gift?" Angeline asked.

"The gift will fade, and they'll be human again. In the process we'll erase their memory and free everyone from this place." Hecate replied.

"What about their mate?" Angeline asked.

"Their mate will get a new mate, and Sage will go on to live a normal human life." Hecate replied.

"Why?" Angeline asked.

"Because Sage has done some horrible things, and they're lucky we're allowing them to live. If they choose not to abide by the rules then we'll have to go a different route with them." Hecate replied.

"I'm convinced that this can be fixed." Angeline said.

"Very well." Hecate said and waved her hand.

Angeline saw her clothes change from the wet clothes she was wearing to a pair of stark white starched scrubs. Her hair was in a tight bun on the nape of her neck and her nails had been shortened to suit the job for which she was applying.

"How?" Angeline asked.

"I'm powerful and magic." Hecate replied.

"What about my life?" Angeline asked.

"Your life has been put on hold. So, when it's time for you to return to your life everything will be as it is now." Hecate replied.

"My job is safe as of now?" Angeline asked.

"Yes, and you'll be putting that to good use as well." Hecate replied.

"Then let's get this done and over with, so I can return to my life." Angeline said.

Hecate raised her hand and snapped her fingers. Angeline was pushed through a forcefield and was standing at a set of double doors. The doors were stolen, and looked like they were surrounded by razor wire.

Angeline took a deep breath and reached up to ring the bell. The doors opened and she stepped through hesitantly. She was greeted by a short overweight woman who had a weary smile on her face.

Angeline gave the woman a polite smile and the woman looked at her with fear.

"Run child and don't look back." The woman said.

CHAPTER SIX

Lovers Meet

Angeline was well versed in the Next Star Rehab's daily routine after being there for what seemed like years. She'd learned how to fit into the staff, and was slowly transitioning Sage from male to female. Sage didn't know it was Angeline's magic that was helping them with the transition.

The day that Sage woke up with no visible facial hair they were in shock. Standing in front of the mirror they touched their smooth face, and smiled. They immediately called out to Angeline to witness the change.

"What's wrong?" Angeline asked.

"Look at my smooth face. Everything is finally falling into place." Sage said.

"What are you talking about?" Angeline asked.

"I woke up and I have no facial hair, and my chest isn't hairy anymore either." Sage replied baring their chest.

"Wow! What's the formula for getting rid of unwanted hair?" Angeline asked.

"No, I'm not just getting rid of unwanted hair, I'm transitioning like I wanted to all those years ago." Sage replied.

"I don't think I understand." Angeline said.

Sage lowered their head and looked at Angeline with sadness. Angeline took their hand and gave them a soothing pat.

"You can tell me anything." Angeline said urging Sage to speak.

Sage let out a sigh and handed her a folder that they kept on the bathroom shelf. Angeline took the folder and waited for Sage to give permission to look through it. When Sage finally nodded their head Angeline opened the folder.

Inside the folder were several pictures, and a lot of medical records. The first picture was of Sage at the age of about twenty years old. The next picture was of a female with the same features as sage, but more feminine. The third picture was of Sage in their current state.

Angeline took the folder and went to sit at the desk in the main room. Sage followed and had something clasped in their hand. When Angeline sat down she spread out the contents of the folder across the desk.

Setting the pictures out in front of her in order Angeline started reading the documents. The first one was a medical plan to transition into a trans woman. The second one was of the actual surgery and how it was botched.

"It says here that your genitalia surgery was unsuccessful. The removal of the penis was done with too much force. How did something like this happen?" Angeline asked.

"I'm not sure how this happened. The way I understand this surgery is that the penis was supposed to be dissected and then tucked to give me a vaginal opening with the urethra attached to the clitoris. The doctor castrated me instead." Sage explained.

Angeline put her hand to her mouth in shock at this revelation.

"How on earth do you even use the restroom?" Angeline asked.

"I have a catheter to drain my bladder." Sage replied.

"Did you sure?" Angeline asked.

"Yes, and I won in court which is how I was able to open this fabulous place." Sage replied.

"Have you tried a new doctor?" Angeline asked.

"No, I built this place and decided to use magic to fix this issue." Sage replied.

"What kind of magic?" Angeline asked.

"I'll be honest with you because you've become a very trusted person in my life. Once I tell you this we have to keep this between the two of us. No one knows anything about what I truly do here." Sage replied.

"I give you my word." Angeline said.

"I'm over two hundred years old. When I figured out that I was mated with another man everything I was feeling clicked. It was frowned upon when I was younger, so I stayed alone until the times changed. As soon as they started doing transition surgeries I was one of the first on the list. Of course, I waited a few years for them to perfect it, but I signed up. That's when I realized I picked the wrong doctor. When I built this place I gathered as many magical, and supernatural creatures as I could in this place. They're prisoners with a good life, but none the less still prisoners." Sage said taking a pause.

Angeline sat quietly imploring him to continue. Sage sighed again and continued.

"If I take a person down into the experiment room then they don't usually come out alive. I've taken vampires, werewolves, and witches down there and I'm finding now that I have to have all three and a little human blood as well to make the spell work. Once I've drained the creature I bathe in their blood and recite the words of a spell my mother gave me." Sage explained.

"Where do you get the human blood?" Angeline asked.

"I hate to admit it, but I lure a human with the promise of a job and then reveal the location. Once I've done that I gain their trust and then eventually drain them. They have a lot of blood in their bodies, so one human can last for several spells." Sage replied.

Upon hearing this Angeline knew she had to work faster on this transition. She couldn't allow another human to be sacrificed for these spells that weren't working. Sage didn't catch on in their enthusiasm that the spell was actually working.

Angeline nodded looking over each of the pictures and the documents knew what she had to do. Sage interrupted her thoughts dragging Angeline from her mental planning.

"What?" Angeline asked.

"Would you like to help me?" Sage repeated.

"With?" Angeline asked.

"I have a very powerful vampire, and some not so powerful witches and dragons that need harvested. I've got to lure a human in the next few weeks, but for now this should work." Sage replied.

"Yeah, I can do that. Who's the vampire?" Angeline asked.

"You'll need help getting him, but he's down in the belly of the third building. His name is Tyson he's over two hundred years old, and he's one step under the alpha. His blood will be rich for this next step in the spell." Sage replied.

"I see, and what about the others?" Angeline asked.

"I've got a dragon in the west wing his name is Felix he's weak hasn't even met his mate yet, so he's ripe for the plucking. I've got a witch name Raven in the north quarters who's bound to be his mate. If I can get them together then he should shift into dragon form." Sage explained.

"I don't understand the shifting. Why would his mate cause him to shift?" Angeline asked.

Sage took a moment and explained how the mate to mate shifting happened. When he was done Angeline had more questions than answers.

"If his dragon form can't come out without his mate then do they share power once mated?" Angeline asked.

"You know, I'm not sure. I've heard that it can happen if the mates accept each other, but I've never seen it happen." Sage replied.

"Sounds interesting." Angeline said.

"Once my spell has taken full hold, I can explore that and do experiments on mates. After everything that's happened to me, I want to make them suffer." Sage replied.

"First, we need to figure this out with the spell. Then we can move on to torture." Angeline said.

"Sounds like an amazing idea. I'm so glad you're on my team Angeline." Sage said.

Angeline nodded and put the documents back into the folder and closed it. Sage waved her along and gave her the wing, door number, and name of the person he wanted her to fetch first. Angeline went to the west wing and her body jolted.

Through the window of the steel door, she could see a man standing there staring back at her. A slow smile spread across his face and Angeline saw his true form for what it was. This was her mate, and she had to protect him at all costs.

CHAPTER SEVEN

Lovers Escape

Angeline opened the door, and Felix knew instantly who she was. A small child appeared next to him, and she was fierce. She tried to push Angeline out of the room, but Angeline quickly explained who she was.

The child held up her hand and bowed to Angeline. Felix did the same gesture and Angeline watched them curiously. When the girl stepped forward Angeline knelt down in front of her.

"Hello, I'm Viola. I'm Hecates ghostly figure." She said.

"So, you're Hecate?" Angeline asked.

"No, I'm someone who was here and sacrificed for Sage's spells. Hecate used a spell to keep me here and watch over the two of you." Viola replied. Since I've been here I've grown attached to Felix we're from the same." Viola explained.

"From the same what?" Angeline asked.

"That's for another time. For now, the two of you have to go." Viola replied.

Without another word there was a loud crash, and we were transported out of the Next Star Rehab. Angeline had no idea where she was at, but she was glad she had escaped now that she'd found her mate.

I knew whatever I was about to face would be okay as long as this man standing here was always at my side. He was everything a girl like me could want in a man. I looked into his deep blue eyes and nodded.

Felix wrapped an arm around my waist and snapped his fingers. We were transported in a flash out of the small cozy apartment to a large mansion like a house. I looked around and felt uneasy.

"Where are we?" I asked.

"This is my home." Felix replied.

"Are you Viola's brother?" I asked.

"Yes, in a roundabout way." Felix replied.

"I didn't turn off my stove and I didn't get to eat." I said.

"I'll feed you don't worry about that, and my clean-up crew is there now to make sure your things are kept safe." Felix replied.

"How did you know where I was?" I asked.

"Viola told me." Felix replied.

"How is she your sister in a roundabout way?" I asked.

"I met her in Next Star probably twenty years ago, and we've been closely connected since that day." Felix replied.

"What? She's an eight-year-old little girl. How could you have met her twenty years ago?" I asked.

"Viola was an eight-year-old little girl twenty years ago when Next Star did so many experiments on her that it ended her life. She's been trapped there since in the same torment, same form, and same hell since. I'm surprised she showed herself to you as quickly as she did." Felix replied.

"I don't understand any of this." I said.

"You're a very special girl Angeline Mystic. I'll explain how all of this works though. First ask the biggest question you have." Felix said.

"Did you tell me that Viola is dead?" I asked.

"Yes, she died trying to set me free." Felix replied.

"So, she's a ghost?" I asked.

"Yes, and she will remain that way." Felix replied.

"What did you mean that she died trying to help you? I think you should start from the beginning and go until this moment." I said, shaking my head.

"As a teenager I was in Next Star Community Project. I was raging mad all the time, and my parents couldn't keep up with me. I'd go from fun loving to dark like a light switch flipping on and off. So, they were approached by this man saying he could help them, and that's how I became part of the project. While I was in there I met little Viola. Her room was across from mine, and she would hum while flipping through books that were brought back to her from the Earth realm. She lived for the days she was brought new books, and the ward we were in loved to hear her humming. She wasn't bad at all; she was just little and could be used for experiments for a longer amount of time as she grew up. They didn't know anything about her kind of creature, so they saw a child, but she was actually a full-grown adult. She was eight in the Next Star years, but she'd already lived eight lifetimes in her own realm. Her people are able to project themselves to be whatever is needed at the time. She needed to be a child to get to the bottom of Next Star's games, and so she was. I called her my little sister because I was protective of her. When she explained to me who she was and where she came from that's when I realized she was here to help the rest of us. Call us the chosen few. So far she's chosen seven women including you it's eight, and at least that many men. She's building something, and you're going to be part of it. The reason she came to you the way she did it is because of how she was able to get out of Next Star." Felix explained.

"So, she's not dead?" I asked.

"Dead in Next Star yes, but alive in her home realm." Felix replied.

"I don't understand that. You're talking in circles." I said.

"You wanted to disappear from your apartment

and fake your own death. Well, she had to do the same thing to escape Next Star. She taught me everything I know about this line of work, and I'm using it to help you. When she came to me tonight it'd been a very long time since I'd seen her. I knew then I had someone very special to protect." Felix explained.

"So, she's alive and well, and not a child." I said aloud, trying to wrap my head around it.

It all seemed very made up, and now I was in the middle of something I couldn't figure out. However, I was safe, and these two beings helped me stay that way. My stomach growled and I felt embarrassed for a moment.

"I'll order take out. From the smells in your apartment, you were working on some kind of seafood dish." Felix said.

"Oh, yes I was making a shrimp gumbo and lobster tails." I replied.

"All of that for one person?" Felix asked curiously.

"Yes, I like to freeze it in portions for whenever I want a hardy soup." I replied.

"Smart and beautiful, I can see why Viola chose you." Felix said.

"Why did she choose me?" I asked.

"We need someone who's one of the angel variety who's also a witch. You fit that in more ways than one." Felix replied.

"A what? An angel witch. How is that even possible?" I asked.

"It's something about the blood that courses

through your veins Angeline. You're an angel, but you're also a witch. I've never seen or heard of another like you. If you'd stayed in the Next Star Community Project then you would have been a commodity. They figured it out and that's why Viola got to you so quickly." Felix replied.

"So, what's next?" I asked.

"Well, your identity has been extinguished. Your death will be confirmed at any moment now." Felix replied.

"How? What?" I asked.

Felix mentioned a swirling circle in front of us and we looked through it like a television. I could see that all of my personal effects had been taken out of the room and replaced with those of someone else. Laying there in the middle of the living room was someone who looked just like me, only I was here.

"Is she dead?" I asked.

"She was never actually living." Felix replied.

"What did you do?" I asked.

"Magic. It's like an illusion of you there, and they'll be able to do everything they need to, but it's not real. We've cast a spell to show them what they want to see. Your body will no doubt be taken to Next Star, and they'll try and find the wings that you told them about, but nothing will be there." Felix replied.

"I hope they enjoy that." I said.

Felix laughed and I watched as the director of Next Star came into the room. He looked over every inch of the apartment and said nothing seemed to be out of order. My death was quickly ruled a homicide even though there was no evidence of it, and the fake note sitting there said I did this to myself. The director wanted my body sent to Next Star.

That's when a woman came into the room and stopped them from moving me. He might have his hands in the biggest project in two realms, but she had more pull than he did. She ordered that he leave the apartment and allow her to examine the evidence. It wasn't long before she found the note and held it up.

"Not a homicide, but a suicide. She'll be taken to morgue, and her body has been claimed by the family." She said.

"Who are you?" He asked.

"I could ask you the same thing, but I doubt you'd tell me the truth." She replied.

"I'm Mortimus the director of the Next Star Community Project, and she's my subject. You have no rights here." He said.

"I'm Rainy, the director, president, or whatever you want to call me of Crystal Crest. This is my realm not yours, and since she died in my realm she'll be kept in my realm. Furthermore, her family doesn't want her body to be used in your project. Now, if you'll excuse me she's already been spoken for." She replied.

Mortimus didn't like this, but he had no choice. If he fought them then he would end up in a prison somewhere in the belly of Crystal Crest. If he let her go then he would end up without his prize pupil. Either way he was going to have to do this a different way.

When they finally left my apartment Rainy took my body to the morgue. The morgue was dark and cold, but the woman who called herself Rainy wasn't who she perceived to be. She waved her hands over my body, and it disappeared.

"Meet Viola." Felix said.

I sat there in stunned silence waiting for what was to come next. The screen went dark, and Felix handed me the takeout he'd ordered. I stared at it in shock, but my body's hunger outweighed the scene I'd just witnessed.

CHAPTER EIGHT

Felix showed me where I was going to be staying until everything was settled. He gave me the few items that I came with, and some that were retrieved from my apartment. I at least had a decent wardrobe even if it didn't match what everyone else was wearing.

I slept like shit that first night. Plagued by dreams that were very ominous. Being chased by dragons, and angels while I was on fire. Everything seemed so real until I opened my eyes.

The light shining through the room showed me that there might be hope. I could smell coffee percolating appealed to my senses, and I looked over at the nightstand. There sat a cup of steaming hot coffee and I picked it up.

That first sip passed through my lips, and I closed my eyes to savor it. I wish I hadn't closed my eyes. The flashes of the dream were there in the, and I felt like I was on fire again.

I opened my eyes and looked down at my skin. There were no signs of blisters, or scars from burns, but I could have sworn that I was on fire. I took a deep steadying breath and knew that this was all just my mind playing tricks on me.

I thought back to the day before and recounted everything I knew that had happened. I was rescued from my small apartment in Crystal Crest and brought here. I didn't exactly know where here was, but I was safe, and I ate.

I was drinking this cup of coffee, and it was piping hot. I did not get into a fight with a dragon, and I was almost certain I wasn't really an angel. Some of this didn't quite make sense to me, but I would figure it out in time.

A knock on the door and someone whisking in grabbed my attention. It was Felix and he was in a suit like an attorney would wear. He was dressed very fine, and the suit made him look dapper. I couldn't peel my eyes away from him.

"Glad to see you awake. I've got breakfast for you, and your new identity." Felix said.

"Okay, will I be allowed to work while I'm here?" I asked.

"Yes, you'll have to be able to support and sustain yourself. I have a place in my department store if you'd like to work there." Felix replied.

"I'm quite tired of the retail life Felix. I know it's a job, but the people, the complaints, and the overall horror of it is just not my line of work. I'd like to find something else since I'm someone else." I said.

"Not a problem. There's other things you can do. There's some call center jobs, some factory jobs, and other things like that. What kind of experience do you have?" Felix asked.

"I catch on fast, and I have some training in various things. I refuse to go back to the land of retail though." I replied.

"I know someone who can use a paralegal. Can you type, do research, and various other tasks?" Felix asked.

"Yes, that all seems simple enough." I replied.

"Then let's get into the office and we can get you trained in that. This place isn't like the Crystal Crest you know. We don't allow people to be miserable, and you have a lot of training to do in order to fulfil your destiny." Felix said.

"What destiny are you referring to?" I asked.

"The one you've been chosen for. You've got a long ways to go before we know exactly what you're capable of Angeline. Once we do find out then we'll be able to train you in that." Felix replied.

"How can you train someone to be an angel who does witchcraft if you've never seen one?" I asked.

"It's all part of the plan, you'll know exactly what you need to do when the time comes." Felix replied.

"Okay, I guess I better get dressed for this day if I'm going to become a paralegal." I said.

Felix sat the breakfast try on the nightstand

where the coffee once was, and left. I got up and dressed in a pair of slacks, a black button-down shirt, and shoes. I looked the part now, but I had to get this wild hair tamed.

After I slipped my hair into a tight bun, I ate the bacon on the tray of breakfast and carried the tray back to the kitchen. Felix gave me a nod of approval when he saw me and announced it was time to go. I grabbed my wallet that had my old identification in it and Felix stopped me.

"This is your new identity. You'll keep your first name, but your last name will change. You're going to be Angeline Christine Colfax, and go by Christine. Your date of birth has changed, so get used to the new one, also your identification number has changed. You'll have to get used to all of this." Felix explained.

I nodded and took the new papers that he gave me. I glanced at the driver's license and wondered why it still had my old address on it, if I was presumed dead. I held it up and scrunched my nose.

"I died here, so why is it my new address, and where exactly are we?" I asked.

"You're going to have to trust me Angeline. I know it sounds crazy, but all of this is for your own good." Felix replied.

"It sounds like a secret I don't want to keep." I said.

"It's a secret you'll have to keep in order to keep you safe." Felix replied.

"Alright, I'm listening. Let's get to work." I said, trying to sound nonchalant.

I knew right away I didn't want to get involved with this dark-haired gorgeous man. I was still worried I was going to be taken back to Next Star and my mind was racing from the dreams. All of this combined made me want to run away and never look back, but I knew it would just follow me where I went.

One thing I did know for certain. Viola was Rainy and had somehow concealed her identity from Next Star, and I was going to do the same thing. When the time came I would reclaim my life and be better than ever.

Today, however, I was going to become a paralegal and learn how to be content with my life. I followed Felix out of the huge house and saw the car to which he was walking.

It was a sports car, and a flashy one at that. If he was trying to conceal our identities this wasn't the way to do it. I looked around and saw that things weren't going as they should be. I could feel eyes on me and was uneasy.

I got into the car and turned to Felix after buckling up.

"Someone's watching us." I said.

"We're safe here." Felix replied.

"I'm telling you we were being watched." I said.

"This is a safe place, and I know you're a little

paranoid after last night. However, this is the safest place in any realm." Felix said reassuring me.

"You're wrong, this isn't the safest place. We're being watched." I replied.

"That'll all settle down in a day or two. Today we're going to find you a place to live. I noticed you brought a considerable amount of cash with you." Felix said.

"You went through my things?" I asked.

"Yes, I had to make sure you weren't tagged or air marked. This place can't be found by anyone by accident or on purpose." Felix replied.

"Well, I have what I need to get into a new apartment, but what happens to my old one?" I asked.

"It's being cleaned and will be rented out to someone else." Felix replied.

"Okay, I want my security deposit back." I said.

"We'll make sure you get it back." Felix replied.

"Thanks, but what do we do about the man standing there in the bushes?" I asked, pointing at a bush where I could see a camera lens.

Felix looked over to where I was pointing and saw what I saw. He got out of the car and was pulling the man out of the bushes faster than I'd ever seen anyone move. I thought my eyes were deceiving me at first, but he had the man suspended in the air about two feet off the ground.

I recognized this man and wanted nothing more than to make him suffer. I got out of the car and walked over to Felix placing my hand on his shoulder.

Felix was glaring at this stranger and then looked into my eyes.

"Set him down Felix I know him, but we're still not safe." I said.

"Who's this man hiding in my bushes?" Felix asked.

"His name is Austin, and we used to date. He's been stalking me since the breakup." I replied.

"How long ago did the two of you part ways?" Felix asked.

"Almost three years ago." I replied.

"Why are you still stalking her?" Felix asked tightening his grip on Austin's shirt.

"Women don't leave me, I leave them. She doesn't get to just walk out of my life and start something with someone else." Austin replied.

"Wrong, you ended things with me when you slept with your employee." I said.

"You should have stuck around until I was ready to let you go Angeline. Just because I sleep with other women doesn't mean that you can just walk out. I wasn't done with you yet." Austin snarked.

"You were done with the me the minute you decided to cheat. Things ended and will remain that way. Stop stalking me, I've moved on." I said.

"I know you're running from something, and they've paid me to keep an eye on you." Austin said, taking a deep breath of air.

"What are you talking about?" Felix asked.

"The one you're trying to hide her from." Austin replied.

"What?" I asked.

"You can't hide from them Angeline. They want you and they knew your death was faked. All I have to do is tell them where you are, and you'll be apprehended." Austin replied.

"Do you honestly think I'm going to give you an opportunity to walk out of here?" I asked.

"You wouldn't want them to all come crashing down on you now would you?" Austin asked.

"They'd come crashing down on you first." I replied.

"That's highly unlikely Angeline; I've got what they want." Austin said.

"No, you think you do, but you don't." I replied.

"Run little errand boy, and tell them where we are. Once they arrive here they'll find nothing just like at her apartment." Felix said.

"We'll see about that." Austin replied.

"I'll make sure that they bring you forward, so I can punish you myself for all of these lies." Felix said.

"You wish. I have proof she's here." Austin replied.

"You have proof you think she's here, but they'll want actual proof." Felix said.

"Next Star Community Project isn't easily fooled Felix. They know the difference in the real deal and a fake one." Austin replied.

"They know the difference in a lie and the truth

too. So, make sure when you go back to tattle like the little bitch you are that you tell them that you were spying on my wife and I while we were preparing for work." Felix informed him.

"She's not wife material, and you didn't have enough time to wife her." Austin replied.

"We were married two weeks ago and we're on our honeymoon Austin. I think you'd do well with the truth now that you've tried to lie." Felix said.

"Angeline isn't married." Austin replied.

"Angeline is married to me." Felix said.

"I didn't know that you two knew each other that well." Austin replied.

"My wife has never been to Next Star, and shouldn't be threatened in her own home." Felix said.

"I know what you're trying to do here, and it's not going to work." Austin replied.

"Good, go, run, tell the masses you found my wife here going to work, and see them all scramble to see her. I'm not afraid of the Next Star Community Project, and I'm not scared of you." Felix said.

"We'll see about that." Austin replied.

Felix released Austin, and then patted him on the head like a dog. I'll be here waiting for you." Felix said, and then snapped his fingers.

I watched them go back and forth and wondered what they were talking about. It was like Felix wanted Next Star to come here, but he was running from them the same as I was. Why would he want them to do that knowing the situation we were in?

CHAPTER NINE

We arrived at the office and Felix sat me in an office by myself. He handed me a laptop and told me to find an apartment. I got busy looking for something to rent. There were all kinds of apartments available, but there were houses that were just as cheap as the apartments.

When Felix returned four hours later, I had a list of places to call. He looked over my list and then looked over the prices. He did a quick search on his phone for each of the houses, and then took a pen to the list. There was one left that he agreed would be okay.

"We can go look at this one, but the rest of these are too cheap." Felix said.

"I don't mind cheap when I've got to figure it out on my salary." I replied.

"You'll be easier to find in a place like that." Felix said, pointing at one of the smaller apartments.

"What's wrong with that?" I asked.

"It's seven hundred a month, one bedroom, and no laundry area. That screams dirty." Felix replied.

"Why does it scream dirty?" I asked.

"Do you want something so cheap that people look at it and see drug addicts, prostitutes, and whores live there?" Felix asked.

"I'm none of those things." I replied.

"Then step it up Angeline. You need something that will give you more than just a roof over your head." Felix said.

"Fine, what you do think about this?" I asked pulling up one of the other listings.

"That's more like it." Felix replied.

"It's twenty-four hundred dollars a month Felix. I can't afford that even if I still had the retail job." I said.

"Let's go look at it." Felix said.

"Why?" I asked.

"Because you need to have the best security in case people come by. This place has a door attendant at every door, and a security team. You need that kind of security right now." Felix replied.

"I can't afford it." I said, through gritted teeth.

"Yes, you can." Felix replied, with the much fierce she had.

"Fine, let's go." I said.

Felix was glad that I had seen things his way. When we left the office he drove fast in his shiny red sports car until we got to the first apartment complex. The guy on the curb nodded his head at us and opened our doors.

Felix handed him the keys and told him it would be a while before we were done. The guy looked at the car like it was a brand-new toy and he couldn't wait to get his hands on it. Felix winked at him, and we walked inside the apartment complex.

The door attendant held the door open for us and we immediately facing a desk with a security guard behind it. He didn't stand to face us when we walked in, but his face turned into a wide smile, and he picked up the phone. Felix and I stood there waiting for a moment and waited.

"Mrs. Pully your two o'clock is here." The security guard said.

"It's only one, so why were they expecting you?" I asked.

"Shh, just let the man work." Felix replied.

I didn't like being hushed and whisked around like I was nothing more than a plaything for Felix. This was all more than I wanted in any phase of my life, and I planned to tell him about it when this meeting was over. Before I got a chance to say anything else a leggy blonde in a business suit came waltzing out of a door that read PRIVATE in black bold letters across the window.

She walked up to Felix with her hands outstretched and he took them. She pulled herself in and kissed him squarely on the lips very passionately. I raised my eyebrows at the two of them and knew this was more than a business relationship, and I was intruding.

When the two of them broke apart the leggy blonde wrapped herself around Felix like a snake and turned her attention to me. She was running her long-manicured fingernails that were shaped like razor blades down the front of Felix's shirt and glaring at me.

"Who's the dame?" She asked.

"This is Angaline Mystic." Felix replied as if he were introducing royalty.

"No, you're kidding?" She replied.

"I'm not kidding at all. Angeline this is Sasha Pully." Felix said.

"It's nice to meet you." I said, and held out my hand.

Sasha looked down at my hand then slid her eyes back to mine. "Charmed I'm sure, but I'm not touching you." She replied, turning her attention back to Felix.

"Why are you here darling?" Sasha asked.

"I need an apartment for Angeline, but it doesn't look like this is the right place." Felix replied.

"Why wouldn't it be? We've got everything any desperate young woman could need. A pool, a gym, the finest kitchen in the city if she can afford to eat in it, and the apartments are gorgeous. Of course, if she can't afford to eat in such a place she can cook for herself." Sasha said.

I could tell that she didn't like me by her tone and

the way she described my financial situation. She didn't know me at all, so why she thought I was so broke was beyond me. Then again I was standing there with Felix, and there was something going on with the two of them.

"Let's allow her to look at one of them, and then we can decide later. She's new to the city, so she doesn't know what exactly she wants yet." Felix replied.

"Actually, I don't think I like this location." I said.

"You do like this location." Felix replied.

"No, I really don't like the location. It's noisy outside with all the city traffic, the smell in here isn't appealing at all, and I get the feeling that it would be safer in the countryside. I'd always be worried that someone was out to rob me if I left here alone." I said, and snarled my nose slightly showing my disdain for the place.

"I think you should at least look at the apartment." Felix said, in a low tone.

"I think if you want to live here that's fine, but I don't." I replied.

"It's okay Felix, she doesn't need to live here. Besides it's out of her range." Sasha said.

"It's actually not out of my range, but I really dislike the city life, and the smell of rotting food turns my stomach." I replied.

Sasha narrowed her eyes at me and Felix grabbed my arm and rushed me out of the apartment complex. When we got to street level I ripped my arm out of his grasp causing his sharp nails to draw blood and walked away from him. He was angry, but so was I. I didn't want him taking me to his lovers and asking for favors, it was beneath me.

Felix was doing everything he could to get me to stop, but I wasn't having it. He wasn't going to treat me like a child and force me to take something I didn't want. He might be the king of this realm, but I damn sure wasn't going to be his kept woman. I had a life before all of this shit, and I would maintain that independence here.

"Luxor isn't the kind of place you can act like that." Felix said when he caught up to me.

"I don't care where we are, you will not treat me like that." I said rounding on him until we were face to face.

Felix was scared for a moment when he saw the fire light in my eyes. I was livid and I wasn't backing down.

"I wasn't trying to treat you like anything." Felix replied toning his voice down.

"You took me to a place where you wanted to show me off. Only you didn't mention that you were in a relationship with the woman who ran the complex. By the way, she's going to be the first person to sell me out when Austin brings down the gauntlet. She's jealous of me even though she thinks I'm poor, and can't do anything for myself. Really Felix, you should pay attention to the company you keep." I snapped.

"Look, I don't know what was going on back there. What I do know is that Sasha Pully is very loyal. She wouldn't do anything that would jeopardize you or me." Felix replied.

"That's where you're wrong. She's your mole, but you're so blinded by her legs, blonde hair, and tits that you couldn't see it. I on the other hand can see right through her to her soul. You've been duped Felix." I said.

"You talk about me, but what about you?" Felix argued.

"What about me?" I asked.

"Your boyfriend was here just this morning trying to take you back, and here you are bringing him up again. Don't you think he's going to hurt you in some way?" Felix asked.

"He's my ex-boyfriend, and the reason I'm here in the first place. He led the evil renegade into my home where you found me." I replied.

"I think Viola was wrong about you." Felix said.

"I think she was right about me and thinking twice about you." I replied.

"Good for me then isn't it?" Felix asked.

"I guess, but I don't need you." I replied.

"If you didn't need me then Viola wouldn't have sent me to you." Felix said.

"Maybe you need me instead." I replied.

"What the hell do I need with a woman who can't see when someone is doing their best for them?" Felix asked.

"You're useless, you stand here taking up for a woman that will stab you in the back the moment she gets a chance and ignore the warnings from the woman who has no ill will towards you. Tell me Felix what kind of spell does she have you under?" I asked.

"I'm not under any kind of spell; I can think for myself." Felix replied.

"Both of you stop it." A voice came through from nowhere.

We both instantly recognized the voice and clamped our mouths shut. She was listening to us argue over things that didn't matter to anyone and yet people were starting to watch. Sasha Pully stood at the entrance of her apartment building watching us closely.

Felix walked to his SUV and held the door open for me. I got in and he closed the door behind me. I could see what Sasha was even from the dark tinted windows that separated us.

Felix pulled away from the curb and I was still clutching my jaw. He was huffing and puffing over his anger when Violet's voice echoed again. I looked around the car and she formed in the back seat as a full-grown woman.

"What exactly did the two of you hope to gain back there?" Violet asked.

"We needed Sasha's help to get Angeline an apartment, but Angeline declined to even look at it." Felix snarled.

"Cut the crap Felix I was watching the whole

thing. Your lust overran your ass in every possible way. That woman is on the phone right now calling on the forces we just rescued Angeline from." Violet said.

"I told you." I chimed in.

"Shut it Angeline. You have to remember that you're one of a kind and they want you. He messed up by telling that horrid woman who you were, but you messed up by exposing your power and seeing through her. Do either of you know the trouble you're in right now?" Viola asked.

"No, but what I do know is this. This man has no idea how to handle a respectable woman. He wants the sexy woman to run his life when she will ruin him. I want no part of this." I replied.

"He's your mate Angeline. You have no choice in the matter, and soon you will see that." Viola said.

"I choose my mate not you." I replied.

"I didn't choose him for you, and he didn't choose you either. This was written in your book when you first thought of." Viola said.

"I refuse to believe that. We have free will, which is what all of this is built on. So, with that I have the will to say no." I replied.

"You might not see it now, but when the time is right you will. As of right now, the two of you need to separate. Take her to this location and she can get an apartment there. When she told you nothing flashy Felix you should have listened to her. You won't get anywhere in this life without her guidance. She knows what she needs and what you need before you do. You will learn this the hard way, and it will be painful." Viola said.

"Life isn't always easy." Felix hissed giving me a glance.

I didn't speak another word to him on the drive to the other apartment complex. When we got there I went inside the office alone, but kept a listening ear on Felix. I didn't trust him and knew he would be my downfall even if Viola didn't see it.

CHAPTER TEN

The apartment helped me get the independence I needed. I used my experience to gain a job at a local diner to sustain me. The word was hard, and the customers sucked with all their complaints, but I was able to make the tips I needed to move forward in life.

Today was a bad day getting yelled at by the boss since a customer complained about my attitude again. All because I would not watch her stuff while she went to the store to get other food for her screaming kid. Am I really supposed to stand in place, and stop what I am doing to babysit?

I quit on the spot and told him to watch the kid and help the mother out while her husband sat there staring at his phone ignoring everything. I had managed to go to further my education while working in that diner and wanted nothing to do with food or retail again.

When I quit I went right to my little cozy apartment and ordered food from the place I just left. Let them see how the better half will live now. The manager had my order delivered and when Felix showed up at the door with my food I froze in place.

I hadn't seen him in over two years, and now he was my delivery driver. I opened the door and allowed him inside my apartment. Felix looked around and sat the order on the dining room table.

"This doesn't look like what I thought it would." Felix said.

"You wouldn't know since you've never been in a place like this." I replied.

"Just because I've never been to a place like this doesn't mean I'm oblivious to what they look like inside." Felix snarked.

"I guess, you go ahead and live in your ivory tower while I slum it in the ghetto." I replied.

"You like living like this because you don't want people to know about you." Felix said.

"I like living like this because I'm not flashy. I don't need all of that stainless steel to prove I'm someone." I replied.

"Yeah, yes, what do you say we get this done and over with. When are you coming to live with me?" Felix asked.

"I'm not living with you." I replied.

"Viola told you already that you're my mate." Felix said.

"What about Posh Polly?" I asked.

"She's just a friend." Felix replied.

"Oh, a friend with benefits." I said.

"I have a past Angeline; you can't expect a man to be celibate." Felix replied.

"I have a past as well Felix, and it's not about celibacy. All of this is about competition. I don't want to be in competition with your exes, or current lovers. It's not fair to me or them." I said.

"No one asked you to be competition with them." Felix replied.

"You took me to your lovers place to find an apartment, do I need to keep saying this?" I asked.

"She's not my lover." Felix replied angrily.

"Fine, not your lover but she's something to you, and I'm not going to sit around and wait for you to choose." I replied.

Felix stepped back exasperated and threw his hands up in the air. He was mad and it was showing on his face. I annoyed at him picked up the remote and flipped it on. My favorite show was on, and I was ready to relax.

Felix sat down on the couch beside me and started watching Hard Ass Pawn Shop with me. I noticed there was a marathon is on, and decided that's what I'm doing for the night even if Felix sits there and watches with me. I was completely done with his lack of knowledge or conversation.

I tuck into my takeout and get into the show. I laughed and ate my fries before I started on the cheeseburger. Felix watched me and when he realized

I wasn't going to offer him any he decided to phone in his own order.

When I finally fall into a dreamless slumber all I can do is smell the food in the room. My stomach growls and I wake up and find Felix crashed out on the floor beside me. I snarled but decided to let him sleep.

When I looked around the room it wasn't what I thought it was. I thought I had went to sleep, but instead I was in a forest with green trees, and a cloudless sky. I looked around the place, and a white light appeared before me.

It sparkles and changes shape into a guy. A very sexy guy with short black hair, spiked, and the prettiest hazel eyes I have ever seen. Built too, but he was not an ordinary guy since cream-colored wings are sticking out of his back.

He smiles at me and says, "We will meet my angel again..." Then he disappeared.

I woke up the next morning disappointed it was just a dream, and all I wanted to do was go to sleep, and see the cute angel again. The angel who is my other half, and knows me better than anyone else. I feel drawn to him, and if only it were instead of a dream.

I needed to know more about this dream guy, but I didn't know how to get that information with him being just in my dreams. Felix stirred and I knew he was going to claim to be my mate again, but I knew this guy in the dream was something more.

I got up to shower and ignored Felix who was trying to rub the soreness out of his neck. I knew that floor was uncomfortable, but I didn't feel sorry for him at all. He came into my home, and I wasn't about to offer him comfort at the moment.

When I got out of the shower I was dressed in a pair of jeans and a comfortable tee shirt. I walked into the living room and sat on the couch, but Felix was nowhere to be found. I was glad he was gone because now I needed to look for a better job and make things happen.

There was a little general store on the corner of the block where I live. The guy who owns it named the store after his son Kyle, and when his son passed away he couldn't bring himself to sell it or leave the store. I decided that since he was the nicest man in the area he might give me a job.

I didn't exactly need a job, but having one would definitely help keep my mind busy. So, I got my combat boots laced up and headed out of my apartment. When I got to Kyle's general store Felix was standing at the counter chatting with the owner Mr. Victor.

"Ah, hello Angeline." Mr. Victor said.

"Hello Mr. Victor, how are you today?" I asked.

"I'm good dear girl. I've just met this wonderful soul, and he reminds me so much of my Kyle." Mr. Victor said.

"He's something, I've known Felix for a while now." I replied.

"Ah, he said you were a good girl, but I already knew that." Mr. Victor said smiling.

"Thank you Mr. Victor. I've actually come to speak with you about something. Do you have a moment?" I asked.

"Yes, please excuse us Felix." Mr. Victor said.

Victor led the way to the back room and closed the door. I sat down in the chair he offered to me, and he sat in the other one. Mr. Victor turned to face me and had a strong worried look on his face.

"What's the issue my darling child?" Mr. Victor asked.

"I was hoping you had a position available, and you'd hire me for it." I replied.

"I see, and do you have experience working in a store like this?" Mr. Victor asked.

"Yes, I..."

"A yes is all I need darling girl. You can start tomorrow at six in the morning and work for eight hours. The pay for you is fifteen dollars an hour. Now, I know that's not a lot, but we can discuss a raise after ninety days." Mr. Victor said interrupting me.

"I accept that, and I'll be here at six in the morning. Thank you so much Mr. Victor." I said.

"I'll start training you in the morning. It will be a beautiful transition." Mr. Victor said.

"Thank you." I said smiling.

"You're welcome." Mr. Victor said.

I got up and left myself out of the small room happy that I was able to secure this job. Felix was waiting in the front of the store when I got up there. Mr. Victor was following behind me, and I walked right out of the store and headed home.

Felix followed right behind me and when I got into my apartment building, he started up with the questions. He wanted to know why I needed a private moment with Mr. Victor. What was so important that it couldn't be discussed in front of him. When I had enough I rounded on him.

"What I do in my life is none of you concern. You made a choice and so did I. Now, I don't know what it is that you want from me, but if you'd leave now I'd appreciate it." I snapped.

Felix left in a huff knowing that I wasn't doing anymore talking or answering his questions. I had to get ready for the next day and find my way through Kyle's general store. I was excited and ready for this change.

CHAPTER ELEVEN

The store was amazing, it had groceries, shoes, jewelry, accessories, clothes, and various departments that deal with the home. I didn't know how extensive it was because I'd go to the grocery part and leave quickly. On my first day I was introduced to the whole store, and I fell in love with it.

Mr. Victor took me around and told me what the tasks were. The hardest part of the job was the closing tasks. All of the products had to be reset on the shelves to ensure quality and quantity were both there. I fell in line and loved it.

After working at Kyle's General Store for a while I finally purchased my first car. I loved how freeing it was for me, and the sense of accomplishment. I got a move on to go to work loving drive on Surrey road the main one in Crystal Crest which is run by psychics. I use the main road to get to the job.

Music blares from my stereo drowning out the

annoying noises of cars, and semi-trucks. I always hate driving at rush hours so close to five. I leave at 4:10 to be there by 4:30. I only have 5 hours this time versus eight.

I can feel people in their cars like pulsing mounds of energy with emotions buzzing like bees. People who are angry, sad, mad, and happy. I grab my opal ring on the rough black dashboard, and put it on the metal making their energy even more numb, so I can't feel their shift. I have a hard time feeling all of that energy, and filtering it through my body to release positive energy.

Doing this routine every single day since moving here gave me a sense of nostalgia. It reminded me of my mother and how she said predictability isn't always a bad thing. It gives us the element of surprise when we switch things up on our enemies.

This thought of my mom got me thinking more about her and my past. My mom never disclosed to me where she got me from. She retold the story of how she adopted me and how I was from a family that was unique. Once I overheard her talking to one of my cousins about some people from her past, but looking back now she was talking about my biological parents.

The male had wings, and the female was a being with strong energy radiating off her. Of course, she was high on weed at the time so maybe she was imagining things. I moved out of my house after I graduated high school, went to community college, and transferred to South Bend to study remotely while training some unknown power I felt within my core.

That's when I found the stones, gems, and crystals that seemed to pop up in various places where I was training. The stones would give me energy, block negative energy, and glow in various instances. I came to rely on them and allow them to guide me through tough situations.

For instance, these stones I am wearing will give me the energy I need to block the various things around me especially seeing Polly enter Kyle's General Store. Out of all the times she could interrupt my life she chose today of all days. We've been busy with the holiday rush, and these stones around my neck, on my finger, and in my ears were in overdrive.

Today is one of the busiest days in retail besides the day before Christmas with people itching to get their hands on the latest gadget, television, tablet, and deals they would not normally have every day. It is the worst day ever since it is usually so full of people that I have to have my stones on or else my brains will implode with their energy.

Polly was sure to cause me mental anguish with her perfectly polished nails and her slicked back high bun. She gave me a sickening sweet smile as she waltzed up to me and drummed her nails on the shelf above me. I smiled at her, but I'm sure she noticed my annoyance.

"Hello again Polly, how can I help you?" I asked.

"Ah Angeline, how kind of you to remember me." Polly retorted.

"You're a hard person to forget. How can I help you?" I asked.

Polly threw her head back and gave a fierce sharp laugh that sounded like it echoed a dark undertone.

"You girl can help me by leaving Felix alone." Polly replied cooly.

"You'd do well to tell Felix to leave me alone, while I continue with my day-to-day life." I replied.

"I've been watching you Angeline, and I know you're calling him to do your bidding. He's a taken man and you need to remember that." Polly said harshly.

"Considering I don't want him; I assure you I could care less about any of this." I replied.

"You're a terrible liar Angeline, but you don't want to cross me." Polly said.

"Do you really think threatening me is the best way to get what you want?" I asked.

"I think that you're standing in the way of something that's bigger than you are." Polly replied.

"I assure you; there's nothing here that I want from you, or Felix. If you want Felix to stay away from me then you should discuss that with him." I said and turned to leave.

Polly reached out with her sharp manicured nails and scratched the side of my neck while grabbing my long ponytail. On reflex I turned instantly and used what I can only describe as a shield and pushed her backwards a full six feet. Polly stood staring at me and the stone on my finger started to glow bright.

I imagine my bodies aura around me, and surround my whole body with metal like a tower blocking everything out. I don't want to feel anything for the moment, and need this to protect me. I hate that I revealed this party of my power, but she left me no choice when she attacked me.

I could hear her thoughts and her facial expressions as she sized me up. I had no fear against her, and it irked that well-polished look she hid behind. She was the definition of true evil, and her thoughts screamed what she was really hiding.

Polly was the creator of Next Star, and she had entered the realm under false pretenses in order to create it. She was jealous of the power each creature she held in that horrible place, and was trying to find a way to drain their power and soak it up to use as her own. However, she underestimated me and what I was truly able to do.

Without another word and that smirk on her face, Polly turned on her heels and clanked out of the store. I looked around and saw the mess I'd made by the force of the shield, and I groaned. I'd not only let my power show unabashed, but I'd left a mess in the wake of it.

I took a moment and calmed myself down and the glow from the ring dimmed down. There wasn't anyone in the area to witness what I was about to do, so I took the chance. I snapped my fingers and the product that fell on the floor was quickly replaced on the shelves and straightened out.

I went through the rest of the store and repeated my actions until each shelf was faced and shaped back up. After a half, an hour of stocking shelves as fast as I could by using magic my relief arrived. He was familiar somehow yet still a stranger.

I gave him the daily rundown and clocked out before I lost control on my power and emotions. I wanted to cry, but I needed to heal the deep scratches in my neck. I really just wanted to track Polly down and show her the same curtesy she showed to me, but I knew revenge at this moment would do more harm than good.

When I got home I imagined a rock around my body, and it enabled me to fully block out everything. Nothing can get through except for my own thoughts in my head. Fully prepared to lose my self-control I threw a shield around my apartment that stopped the sound from escaping and relented.

After exhausting myself I collapsed on the floor of my living room and wept. That poor child and the other children who were tortured under Polly's fake rouse to help are gone now. I couldn't get to them or save them, and it was hurting me deeply.

I could feel their pain after hearing the truth. I could see the fear on their faces. She was the real monster here and she needed to be stopped. I didn't know how or when, but a well thought out plan is what it was going to take.

CHAPTER TWELVE

I get to work to see the front already busy with customers waiting to get in. They've got shopping standing in line outside of the door like it wasn't starting to snow. I open the front doors and the lights flip on. I know immediately that Mr. Victor is there and ready to take on the day.

It wasn't long before the people started pushing their way to the front to checking out. The ringing of the items being passed across the register at self-checkout was passing faster than the register could keep up, so I knew items were missed in the checking process. I take deep breaths as I pass by people, and nearly get hit by a man not paying attention to where his cart is going.

In his haste to get by me he snarled and hissed at me. I was not in the mood to deal with his attitude on top of my already hyper emotional state. I was focused on the job and people who were rushing, and he was not my priority.

That's when I heard his response...

"Whatever. Fuck you too." He said and got in line.

I make my way through the crowd ignoring the remark and I'm stopped by someone else.

"How much is this?" a man asks.

"Does it have a sticker price?" I ask wondering how this was missed.

He looks at the item in question, "Yeah, it says $5."

"That's it and it's priced as marked." I reply trying not to hide my annoyance.

The customer is always right bullshit is what I remind myself every time someone asks me a pricing question when it's clearly marked. It makes me sick because nine times out of ten they don't know their heads from their asses. I make it a point to ignore it all. I pass by everything to get to the fitting room to check for locked doors when I notice the man who almost hit me with the cart earlier watching me.

I do my best to ignore him, but I notice that the bracelet I'm wearing shines a deep hue of red in his presence. I'd never seen the stones, crystals, or jewels I have glow quite that deep before. At first it alarms me, but I chalk it up to the anger he expressed earlier towards me.

I continue to ignore and walk through the rest of the store. When I finally run into the temporary employees that are gathered in the freezer section and wonder what they're doing standing around. I completely forgot about some of the workers they don't know what is going on, and I needed them to get on the ball.

I notice there's a shipment of product sitting in the middle of the freezer section where the new hires are and roll my eyes. They've let people rifle through the merchandise and open the boxes. There were smashed boxes and damaged products now and the person that was hired to supervise these people were nowhere to be found.

I noticed they were grabbing enough to fill their shopping carts, not leaving any for other nice shoppers to buy it. We were having a blowout sale for black Friday and things were priced to move. The sale was $5 for five shirts. $1 for one item, some grab enough to clothe a family for four years, and then return it the next day just because.

Greedy bastards in my opinion buying stuff they don't need all because of a stupid store sale that comes once a year. I hate it. Dealing with people sucks this day. I make my way through the flood of people crowding the store like fish in a stream, or more like zombies in a horror movie not after flesh.

The questions I get asked on the way there are laughable. Is this for sale? Is this discounted? Is this really the price? No, it is just a random number we put on there to confuse the shit out of you. If it were in the sale there would be a blue sticker if not it's obviously not on sale. No, you can't get a discount since you want to be an asshole about it. It is the price what else would it be a dildo? Seriously, people are that stupid here. I directed another customer to an item when it was right behind him.

I finally get the new hires situated and return to my station only to have a huge pile of reject clothes no one wants to buy. Ones they have tried on, but it didn't fit. Or they just leave clothes in a random spot because they are too lazy to put them back where they found it.

Great! I sort through the wonderful piles of shirts, shoes, socks, underwear, and other articles of clothing to make it easier on everyone. Some awesome people took items out of the packages, and left them on pegs. Bastards. This is not how I wanted my day to go.

An old lady who looks like she could bake cookies and then poison you with them all in one-shot asked, "Do you have this item in green?" She holds up the item in her hand.

I looked at the item, which is a plain black shirt, and one of the black Friday items. I take the item from her and search for it amidst all the grabbing while trying really hard not to hit people with their own stupid full carts. I find display with it in hand, and search for the item it is not going to be there since it's sold out.

I go back to tell her the dreadful news,

"Nope, no green all that is left is black, red, and pink."

Her face falls then she smiles, "Well, can you check in the back because maybe not everything is out yet?"

I sigh, "The items in the back are all on the sales floor."

She glares, "Thanks anyway for being a lazy employee." She walks away.

It makes me tried to hear that people think we have a magical back when we don't. Our backroom is filled with overstock items which are binned. I continue folding clothes at a table ravaged by customers. I got half a side done.

A few minutes later I saw a lady come up to the side I just straightened, and she took a shirt unfolded it and left it there. Looking through for her size and wrecking everything else in the process. She did it to every single shirt on the straight side, and did not have the decency to put it away.

I grudgingly refolded the side and finished the other side wanting to strangle the lady with the shirts. They were in a messy heap on the floor, and I fixed them like a good drone would. Giving a glare her way.

"Hey, Angel you finally made it?"

I smile when I hear that voice I know all too well to whom it belongs.

Kalisa Stryker my light at the end of this shitty retail tunnel. Also, my best friend, and one I can vent to at a bar at the end of a long, shitty workday full of assholes.

"Yep, I did though I wish I hadn't since a nice customer went and messed up my hard work…"

Kalisa has wild auburn curls, yellowish green catlike eyes, and green eye shadow with a poison Ivy leaf at the end of her corners. She even has cherry plump lips that will make guys fall to their knees. She is pale like the full moon shining brightly in the sky.

Kalisa does not take shit from anyone, and she loves people. She always has a smile for me, and any man dumb enough to fall for it. I have been friends with her since middle school, and I really love the fact that she is not a mindless Kyle-kissing drone.

I swear some of the employees must have sucked his dick to get the promotions they got. Or Salem did to get promoted to stupidvisor.

"Good. We need to stick together on the battlefield with zombies scrambling for sales."

Her eyes widen when she sees the mess the customers left, "Fuck me. The piggies are out in drones today. That is the sixth fucked up pile of items I've seen."

I smile sadly, "It won't be the last on this hellish day."

We begin picking up the pile the customers tore through like a lion through a gazelle. The jerks. I hate it when they do that. It wastes my time when I have to pick up every individual piece, refold it, and put it back neatly then it's messed up all over again.

Awesome day! I just hope I don't have to watch the phones they are a pain in the ass more than anything. Apparel people are trained to watch phones since it is a part of the job. As well as putting up stock, putting things back, and watching the fitting rooms and phone.

The only reason phones can be a pain is because sometimes people don't answer the phones in their department, and the customer gets mad at us. Everything is my fault just because I work there. I get everything done in an hour, and it is still crowded as I fought my way through the hordes of people.

People are getting mad over not getting a pair of jeans since we ran out the ones mentioned in the ad. I really wish I were somewhere else because the energy they give off is hard for me to deal with when it is beating down on me like an echo in the room.

After I was done the supervisor Emma found me amidst all the craziness. The supervisor is a woman with long brown hair to her ass, wide black eyes, and pale skin like sunlight that fell from heaven. She wore the uniform that curved to her body versus fought it like mine always does.

She had an earpiece in her ears connected to the walkie to listen in on idiot managers. She is actually one of the good managers who loves her job too unlike some of them who sit there and bitch and don't do jack shit to help their sales associates. She smiled at me, and it was the wicked one that told me that one of my worst nightmare is coming true.

"Since you're done with that task I would like to have you man the jewelry counter with Dreama since she needs help while Jasmine is on her lunch." She gives me the keys, and I take them from her the little metal keys opening the cases, and showing the zombies the merchandise.

I smiled at her even though I wanted to tell her no, and to do it herself. I hate the counter as much as I hate the register. Kyle always hangs around the front and hollers when there is no one at the counter.

"No problem only an hour right? How bad can it be?" I said using fake enthusiasm.

I make my way there only to see it is already busy with nonstop humans at least they found all the items since they did not have it earlier.

My thoughts immediately go to, "Great! Thanks bitch for making me face the firing squad or stared at like a zoo animal.

Dreama spots me her blue eyes sparkling like I saved her from dying. Her long black hair in a ponytail curled to her back, and she is tan from the beach. The uniform is perfectly molded to her body like a second skin making her curves stand out.

I got the extra keys from Emma, and head behind the counter to tag team with Dreama to thin the lines down. I serve a few people by showing them pieces and ringing them up when they are satisfied. It is not too bad things are going well until a guy comes up to the counter and clears his throat.

"Can you put a battery in my watch?" He asked.

I take the watch and examine it noticing it is not one of the brands we carry inside the store. We don't take the batteries out unless we carry that particular brand. By following this small rule, it keeps us from getting frivolous lawsuits after the customer claims we've broken their watch.

I regretfully say, "Sorry, sir due to liability issues I cannot open this watch since we don't carry it in store."

He glares, "You have done it before that is why I knew to come here." He snaps.

"I can't open it since it's not a brand we carry." I repeat since this asshole is not getting it.

He stares me and I can hear his thoughts. He's seriously about to sue Kyle for the watch when he claims we've broken it.

"Get me Kyle." As if he can make me work on it when I'm not getting fired over an asshole's watch.

"I'm here already sir. I saw you yell at one of my associates like a jerk." Kyle replies appearing out of nowhere like managers do.

Of course, there is always the talking of the walkie if it not in their ears, and the jingle of keys can be heard too.

"Now what seems to be the problem?" He asked in a friendly tone even though he is a ruthless douche that fires without warning.

"Well," he glared at me clearly trying to intimidate. "This worker refuses to open my watch she says, and I quote "no, I can't this is not one we carry" and due to liability issues. I just want a battery for my watch." He gives Kyle wide eyes as if he can get his way.

"Unfortunately, it is true due to an associate messing up a watch that we did not carry. We had to pay for it to be repaired." He replied apologetically.

The customer sighed, "Then how do I get it fixed?"

"Go to the mall I'm sure they have plenty of places there." Kyle informed him.

"Okay, I guess I will leave." Then he left the counter.

Kyle walked away to bug someone else, and get on their ass about something stupid. That was fun! And it ends like that sometimes, and sometimes the customer is not an asshole about it.

I serve several more customers, and Jasmine comes back. She is a pretty caramel skinned woman with smiling brown eyes. She has long charcoal locks that have a mind of their own. She comes up to me, and I hand her the keys then go back to my section.

Emma finds me yet again and says, "The lines are too long, and you and Jasmine are needed at the front."

"Nooooooo! Oh, the horror! Not the front register! I'll do anything else." I said.

The first thing I hated about being register trained was being called to the front because people there suck. It is too fast, and there are too many brains for me to handle. Not to mention they are rude to the cashiers, blame everything on them, and treat them like they are stupid.

Black Friday also means lines up the ass and curving around everything I walked up to the front noticing the people in line are glaring at me like it's my fault the lines are long. They always seem to look at the sales associates who are putting up stock when they are waiting in line with such venom just because they are not up there servicing their every whim.

The lines are now so long they are past the counter, and some are getting so impatient that they try to check out at another register like the jewelry, electronics, or sporting goods. I go to a customer service manager to get the dreaded register number since they are numbered 1-40. It is a big store, and it all lit up thanks to Black Friday.

The customer service manager Melissa who has long, wavy light brown curls, and light brown eyes that can see right into your soul since she is suspicious of everyone. She wore the uniform like it was a second skin. She had the attitude to direct cashiers as if they were soldiers going onto the battlefield against an army of mindless shoppers.

They are mindless and their eyes are glazed over while they look at the stuff in their shopping carts. I make sure she spots me, and resist the urge to hide in a clothes rack so she can't see me. I got my register assignment and took a few deep breaths before I put my customer service smile on.

I know this whole line is about to shift to me

because this register is closest to the door, and everyone always goes to because they know I'll get them out of here faster. In my head the death march is playing in my head because I fucking hate it

I plaster a smile on my face, and imagine them dead. I get up to the dreaded register, punch in my keys and yell, "I'm open.."

Even though I know some of them will ask if I'm really open with my light on. They advance like zombies to my register taking merchandise and putting them on the rotating belt.

One lady says, "Bout damn time I have been waiting forever!"

I grab her items, and pass the barcode over the scanner hearing the beeps as the items scans. Then after it beeps and appears on the screen time to bag! Fruits and vegetables are together. Dairy is separate as well as meat since meat can leak out everywhere contaminating everything. All the crushed items go in a separate bag like bread and chips. I always put eggs in a separate bag and give them to them. Lastly, no mixing chemicals with food either since you don't want them to get mixed up and spill on something. I double bag wine and cans. I try to talk to the customer in front of me as I bag her items. But I get done, and then tell her the total.

"Ma'am your total is $179.28." I say waiting for her to pay.

Her eyes widen, "You can't be serious I thought it would be less..."

It adds up especially when you don't keep track of the money you are spending.

"Taxes make it higher to keep the creatures at bay, and we wouldn't want a werewolf eating the dogs now would we?" I replied cheerfully since we have taxes in the Crystal Crest realm high to help please the supernatural's by paying them to live in the Luxor realm so they can let us be at peace. But I would love to meet one. I don't fit in with the people here at all. And this woman makes me wish I had a zombie nearby.

She glares, "Then let me take something off. I can't believe these freaks make our taxes high it's bad enough the monsters under our bed are real."

She looks at the items already in the bag, and gives me enough items to void till the total was to her liking.

"Your new total is $70.00." I say with an exasperated smile.

She smiles, "Thanks but you could have been nicer." Turning me from sweet to bitchy in 2.5 seconds because they treat the people behind the counter like dogs. Or servants. Bitch…This is why I hate the register the people suck and treat you like shit.

"Yes, maybe but you need to factor in tax before you jump down my throat for something I can't control."

She glares again turning from sweet to bitchy, "You need to learn manners."

"Whatever take your shit and stop arguing with me over stupid tax dollars." I fired back.

She takes her bags after I give her the receipt, but not before I erase the memory of me being mean and give her new ones. I do it because people like her complain all the time, and I've had this ability since high school when I wanted to erase a moment that has happened like the school bully laughing as I slip on paper.

I have powers and I use them for fun. One day I can find someone from there to see why I have all these powers, and I can't go there because only a supernatural creature will be able to feel the entrance to the realm and know its location.

After the wish of a customer left the people after her are nice, and it almost makes me hate the register less. Then I deal with another one that made me wish I could program them to jump off a cliff.

I scanned his items, and told him the total.

His eyes narrow at me as if I offended him by the total, "Wait, that's supposed to be 2 for 2 not $4.00."

One of those guys...

I give him my fakest smile even though I wanted to wring his neck, "No problem, sir I can fix it."

I meant to hit the void button, but I accidentally hit the enter. "You charged it again." Thanks asshole for pointing out my flaws.

"I told you I can fix it sir you don't need to treat me that way." I tell him since he is being a real dick about it.

I think about how to make it so it shows up that way, and he's giving me looks like he doesn't think I can do the job.

"Aren't you supposed to know how to do your job?" he asked me.

I wanted to tell him off right then and there and decided I needed this job. I had to add it up and math is not my strong suit. I put it at $1.25 since that'll work, and tell him. "$2.56." he gives me change and I put it in the register.

"You're supposed to give me back $8.00."

"I know that you rude shit head."

I give him his change and say, "Thanks for the attitude when it's not my fault the register never showed the adjusted price."

He glared at me, "Watch your mouth or else I will have your job."

"Take it asshole being fired is better than dealing with idiots like you." Then I fucked with his mind to make him be nicer to people behind the counter.

I turn around and there is a cashier to relieve me of this spot in hell. I'm happy not to be permanently there since I hate it. It felt like an eternity dealing with disgruntled people..

I go back to apparel only to have this lady in a motorized scooter flag me down like a dog.

"Where is there a price checker?" and she repeated her question again like she thought I was deaf..

I take her to the jewelry checker, and scan the

belts. "How is it full price when it was in the clearance section?" she asks me as if it was my fault it was ringing up full price.

"The belts are mixed in together there is sale price and clearance price items mixed in." I tell her.

"Well then shouldn't it be moved to a different section there was 20 of them."

I repeat the same thing.

"I don't think you are understanding me it should not be mixed in with the clearance items." She said treating me like a dumbass once again.

"I do understand you they are mixed in, and it's not my fault because if it were clearance there would be a red tag. I know how to do my job bitch." I tell her not playing nice because of how she is treating me.

"Wow...okay." She replies and rolls off hopefully into traffic where she will get run over by a car.

I make it back to the fitting room since that is where we have the clothes no one wants after they are done trying them on. I check in the baskets to see the clothes, and gather a few of them. I start to put them in their spots.

While I hung up a shirt I spotted Kyle doing his usual walk around the store. To my horror he spots me.

"Good morning." Even though it is 6:00 in the bloody evening.

I smile back a fake retail smile, "Hi, to you too sir. I hope you enjoy your day."

Once I acknowledge him he walks away. Whatever. I have already tried running away. He caught me so that was a bust. I was taking away the trash.

Then I heard the cries to the register after the lines kept backing up. I ran to put away the trash, so I could get up to the front. I saw Kyle, and ran the other way hoping he did not see me.

Instead, he pulls me into the office to accuse me of running away from my responsibilities. Nope, I didn't run away to hide from the register. He just loves to put me on it since he knows how badly I hate it.

In reality he's a power mongering dick and why I wish I could quit. I can't because I need this job to be able to hone in my power. Working retail is hard with all their feelings buzzing in my brain.

Doing this job makes me wish I was like normal a person. That I did not feel them at all. Their misery and pity is enough to make my head pin. The register is the only part of the job I hate since you stand there, and gives me no space to try magic.

I prefer the sales floor, and I also hate the rude customers. I don't take shit from anyone even if the idiots in charge frown upon it. I jump for joy when I go back to folding bliss since it allows me to fold on autopilot and allows me to daydream about leaving.

CHAPTER THIRTEEN

The crowd died down which means I can fold without someone messing it up. I look at the clock and realize that it's almost seven in the evening, and I've worked a double shift. I needed a break and decided it's time for me to clock out and go home.

Kalisa comes back, "The fuckers pulled me too, and if they hired more cashiers this would not have to happen. We need to be on the sales floor doing our stupid jobs."

She trails off, but I know how she feels since I hate it too. I fold, and go back to the fitting room to get all the clothes put away. I tell Kalisa I'm leaving and need to rest before I actually scream what I'm thinking at someone. She laughs at me, but knows I will lose it if one more customer tells me how stupid I am.

I take off my name tag and head to the back. Halfway to my final destination in this store and a customer pulls me aside. Like usual they have nothing else better to do than to annoy the shit out of me.

"Do you work here?" He asked in a confused tone not realizing I'm not wearing a name tag anymore.

I look at him dead in the eye with my eyebrow raised, "Am I wearing a name tag?"

"No, but you are wearing the uniform...so I thought you did."

"Then I'm on break, and I don't work here till I put back on my name tag."

"Then can you get someone not on their break so I can find the price of the item?"

I look at the item in question, and it clearly has the price labeled on it. "It says it right here...use your eyes and stop being lazy."

He glares, but I don't care. I don't even bother hearing his reply. I'm too tired to deal with anyone else and I just want to clock out. I just want to leave instead of listening to this complaint. I went to the time clock and clock out the minute he turned his attention to something else.

I make my way to the back door and escape through it. I knew if I walked back onto the sales floor I'd be bombarded again. That's when I ignored my name being called over the sound system.

Ignoring the repeated pages, and I slipped into Ginger's shop just three doors down from Kyle's General store. She is a local witch or. She is a new age human who loves oil and incense.

I have known her since I started purchasing the

stones from her. She knows about me being able to fool people. She is the one who suggested which stones to use. I come to her when I'm feeling overwhelmed and need something to sooth me until I calm down.

I park my car, and the cool air greets me wishing I had more on. It is now four right now and I have till five for my break. I open the rough door, and the bell jingles. Once I step in the smell of incense calms me, and I recognize the calming chamomile scent.

Yum. It calms me down making my problems melt away. I love the smell, and it makes my stress from asshole Kyle melt. I hate it there, and I have no choice thanks to me wanting to go to a university in Crystal Crest for psychology. I want to study the human mind. I see Ginger behind the counter her green eyes lighting up into a smile on her face when she sees me.

"Hey, how have you been?" She asks noticing the relaxed look on my face.

I smile, "I'm alive aren't I? It has been a hectic Black Friday shift. I just need to get out of there before their energy drains me."

"Do you want me to cleanse you from it?" she asks since she knows it can put a damper on my day when dealing with their negative energy. I can feel the weight of the customers bringing my energy level down. Just like theirs every time they come into the damn store.

I nodded, "That'll be good. I will like it, and I'm going to need it to get through the rest of the shift."

"Yes, I know you need it since you're naturally sassy, but their energy can build up to the point where it can overload your system. Follow me."

I follow Ginger to the back of the store to her cleansing room. I love the smell in this room, it's filled with lavender and verbena.

There is a chair in the middle of a circle with candles. I sit on the chair watching the candles flicker and sway then close my eyes. Ginger puts her hands on me mumbling the chant to cleanse me while lifting the negative energy blocks the customers left in their wake.

They send their energy toward me every time they yell, and it's a horrible blast of energy putting a damper on my day. It lifted off me and I can breathe now. It burns at some point as a person left their hooks in my aura. Negative people use hooks to feed off your life force without doing it, and the fucker must be Kyle.

He has been on my case ever since I started working there a year ago. Luckily, it is fall break, so I don't have to worry about employees until school starts back up again. She stops five minutes later, and I get off the table.

She smiles at me, "Feel better?"

I nodded, "Good as new since I had no idea Kyle had his hooks on me till now. I'm happy I can finally breathe now."

"It was a nasty hook too with barbs coming in showing he was a real piece of work."

"I bet he has had it out for me since day 1."

"There is something I want to ask you though, and a question I haven't asked you before. Do you believe in angels?"

My eyebrow rose, "Like halo, wings, and the things you meet when you die?"

She laughs, "Not like that but they do have wings. They live in a realm separate from ours like in the Luxor realm. Or course, you do need to fly to get to certain places, or ride the friendly angel dragons."

"Okay, why did it not happen before?"

"Not the right time, and if one angel can see what you are then the rest will follow. The dark one Zackary will too, and they will try to steal your powers to escape Hell."

My mind tries to process what she says, but it's too much right now. "I have to go this is too much right now..." I leave the room, exit the store, and head to my car. Work is on my mind now, and I can't deal with this right now...

CHAPTER FOURTEEN

My world has been turned upside down. I can't believe it or process it...I thought I was a person who can sense feelings. Not someone who belongs to an angel. Damn, how did I get so lucky?

This will lead to a way that will let me get out of my miserable job and do something that matters. My head goes back to the dream with the sexy winged guy. My 21st birthday is soon. Like a few days from now.

I make it to Kyle's General Store to clock in after I have time to myself. I really have no idea what I am going to do. None. I clock in choosing not to think about it till it actually happens. At least there is a possibility of getting out of this horrible human-range job. I go to the fitting room, and start putting back the clothes while picking up items customers tossed carelessly on the floor after they didn't want them.

Kyle walked around the store like he usually does, and spotted me. "Good morning."

I nod, and he walks away continuing his rounds like a general or douche in charge. Or dictator. He was with his usual lackey Veronica. The bitch assistant manager everyone hates because she sucks Kyle's dick on a daily basis.

Her dirty curls bob as she walked with him, and her grey eyes give me a cruel icy stare. Her friend Tawny was walking with her, and the blonde had an issue with me too since she told my manager that I was one of the ones laughing about the lack of coverage since the managers suck at scheduling people. She was cruel too. Bitchy Veronica treated me like a dog. I hated her, and I wish I could burn her hair off her dry soulless head,

She yells at me for the dumbest thing ever. "I thought I told you to get a cart." she said not realizing I did get a cart, and it's out of the way. She uses people like her packing mule giving the people under her carts piled high with shoes.

Old lady customers are the worst. They treat you like a servant, and expect you to do everything for them. It was a struggle for one of the jewelry girls to tell an old lady her order was not there since she kept not understanding it. Then an old lady tells one of them to take the plastic holders keeping the watches in place off.

Then there is the old man who yelled about having to take his non-Kyle brand watch to another store after yelling about getting a manager as if they can solve everything. I hate retail, and I hope to God the witch thing is actually true so I can get out of this awful place.

I continue straightening the racks, and making sure everything is off the floor. A customer flags me down, "Do you have any more of these in the back?" She holds up a pair of shirts exclusively for Black Friday.

"Are those the only ones in the area?" I asked her if she wanted to hit her for being so stupid.

"Yes, there isn't any more left, and I need it in a size medium 8-10."

I gave her a sympathetic look, "I'm sorry since we only get a limited amount of those shirts for the event once we run out then we are out."

Her look turns to one of hatred, "So you won't check in the back for me?"

"No, ma'am since this is all we have for the event everything is out."

"Thanks for nothing." She spits making me wonder why I can't slap her because of how rude she is.

No wonder why I hate working here because the customers are just rude pieces of shit. Stupid bitch it's not my fault we are out yet it's still taken out on me. It's not a big deal since I've dealt with it for two years. I begin straightening out the area near the jewelry department cleaning the racks when this happens.

"Get me a manager then this is ridiculous. I paid $5,000 dollars for this watch, and you won't even do it. That is disgusting. You won't do it because you won't carry it? I have had it done here twice already."

I look over to see Jasmine the jewelry sales associate explain why, and the guy is not having it. This is not the first time. She leaves to get the dumbass a manager, and that is when I have a little fun. I say fuck it because if I really am that special I'm not wasting any more time at this shitty job.

I'm quitting and finding something that does not want to make me hang myself every time I come in. I have not done this in a while, so I look at him and deliberately swallow his anger. It doesn't make me feel it at all.

It is an interesting ability to swallow one emotion, and put in a new one. It's like taking an old card, and replacing it with a new one. I made him feel happy, and the guy now has a grin where his scowl had been, and walks away.

I will go elsewhere now, and leave her alone. It's not her fault anyway.

His thought rang in my head, and I could read his mind as if he were speaking to me. Ginger was telling the truth. But what am I? If that's the case I might not be human at all, and that comforts me more than anything knowing I'm not like them.

I smile for the first time ever thinking I might have overreacted. Jasmine comes back with a manager, and lifts up her hand when she couldn't see where he went. I turn my mind back to the task at hand and shield my mind back to keep their thoughts from interfering with my emotional state.

I can block them and unblock them at will. It comes in handy especially during crowded holidays. I thought I was going crazy in high school when I heard thoughts, and their mouths never moved.

It was really hard till Ginger found me, and taught me how to block it out till high school. That's why it hurt so bad when she waited to tell me. Unless she told me because I did not have the dreams till now.

I continue with the mindless tasks of zoning and cleaning after I was finished with the baskets, and I know there will be more the next day. I'm always working there, and people always dump shit in the most random places.

People mess it up all the time perfectly neat tables, and then the next minute messed up since they don't bother to refold the shit they looked at. All the time I find meat in places where it should not be. I even find stolen items stuffed on shelves behind other items.

It's hard not to get discouraged working here since it shows you how horrible people can be toward retail workers. I clock out when my shift is over, and head to my apartment. The day had been long and full of idiots.

My home is the one place I can go to for peace and quiet. No emotions or buzzing thoughts just silence. I've heard so many thoughts today about coupons, Black Friday, and sales that I would rather watch mindless television and not think about anything else for a few days.

I take off my uniform and dress in a pair of blue jeans and a T-shirt. I take off my sneakers in exchange for a pair of slippers to let my throbbing feet rest. Standing on your feet for with hours a day is not easy.

My back and shoulders ache too, and it's pretty hard and draining work. Time for me to settle down and forget about all those assholes that I dealt with today. To forget...To relax and not think about work at all.

I love my small one-bedroom apartment with bathroom, living room, dining room and a small kitchen. I get a snack, and sit my ass on the couch watching television.

The hours go by fast as I watch television drowning out the noise in my own head. I can feel the malachite box my mom bought me before she disappeared. It held a stone that I didn't wish to experience in the end.

Normal might as well be a pipe dream for me if what Ginger said is true. Normal people don't have superpowers like I do. They can't influence people's heads or get into them. None of it, and I can. That's why I have to find out why this angel thinks I am his mate.

The next day I have it off since they made me work Black Friday. I love days off since it means I don't have to deal with the annoying general public who are too stupid for their own good.

I get dressed in a comfortable red short sleeved shirt and blue jeans. I put on my white sneakers since they are a must since I love the weather. My birthday is in two days, and luckily that day I have plans with my best friend Kalisa who has been through hell with me working retail.

She is awesome. She has had my back more times than I can count. I've had good times with her. I head to take a walk and clear my head. After I get outside my hair stands on its end.

I got a sinking feeling like something was watching me. I walk to the park which is less than five miles away. I don't take my stones since it's not crowded as much today since people spent yesterday spending money.

I can use this time to think, and be free of cock sucking Kyle. I walk more noticing the warm air, and thank god it's in the 70's. I love those in between temps. I say fuck it and amp up my pace.

I turn it into a joke, and run like hell. I run until my legs burn in protest, and run like zombies are chasing after me. I hope it's not my stupid ex David Hall chasing me because I told him no being with him since he tried to cheat on me with my friend just to be closer to me, and said he fell for her instead of me. She had a boyfriend, and thought he was a creep too.

I can't have him stalking me like this, and his

thoughts aren't easy to influence and pin down like everyone else's.

Running...to forget the pain he caused me every time he lost my number...running from every time he lied to me about who he was...keeping things from me like the fact that he was a horrible person that forced himself on someone. Running away from wanting to have him move in with me to my apartment, we were talking about marriage, but he hurt me.

It was so hurtful I dropped out of college because he messed me up so bad. So bad I'm taking off a semester from it, and the memories of the guy before him Jordan Simon I was going to be married to him, but he turned into a controlling jerk telling me what to do and how to act.

Telling me he will raise our children a certain way, and I got away we were dating for three and engaged for one. I could never allow anyone telling me what to do. I'm too strong and independent for it. My mind is clear.

I need to find out more, and since I want to drive I head back in my car to go to Ginger's shop. I had to find out more at this point because I have had it with Kyle at this point since he has been terrorizing the staff with his good mornings when it's not even mornings, and riding their asses like a duck.

All that is missing is a whip. I made it to the shop after avoiding an accident when a dick cut in front of me like an asshole. I park the car and head inside. I open the door to her shop and hear the tinkle of the bell as I walk in. I scanned the shop looking for Ginger, and not only did I find her.

She is talking to someone. My eyes met his eyes, and I was lost since he is incredibly hot. My heart beats fast when he smiles at me. The thing that stopped me in my tracks? He had fucking wings coming out of his back. What the fuck is going on?

A guy with wings is not something you see every day. Ginger walks around from behind the counter and smiled, "I was hoping you would come see me."

CHAPTER FIFTEEN

The way Ginger said that made me take pause. I had no idea who these men were, and they were here waiting for me as though they knew I'd show up today. I put up my mental shields and give them a tight smile.

"OH?" I questioned.

"We were too." Three guys comes through the door. They have creeps written over their faces. Spiked black hair, black lizard eyes and black wings coming out of their backs like evil angels.

I feel like I'm in a bad good versus evil movie. The leader of the group smiled at me beaming sharp, spiky teeth. Yuck. A part of me wanted to run away, and the other part of me wanted to slap the smile off his ugly ass face.

"We saw her first, and she is ours now." The incredibly cute guy said.

He was a looker too with long brown hair, and

sexy dark brown eyes that can see into my soul. His muscles flex as he tenses up, and the leader just laughs.

"Really? Do you think your pathetic self can take on deadly assassins?" He snarled.

We are the ones who need her power the most to keep the boss happy before her birthday, so we'll stop yet another half-breed from ruining the races."

"There are others like her, and she is just one of many."

My eyebrow rose at that. More like me? Ginger was staring at the guys who entered the room, and I was just trying not to shit my pants in fear. I drop my shield since it's not like I'm a normal human, and that is where it gets weird instead of seeing a normal human brain activity it's just balls of light and energy. Ginger's is a ball of orange energy too.

I shake my head with the images. I want to break the tension in the room. "What is going on?"

They all look at me and the evil leader spoke, "You're an Angel Witch hybrid that comes to full power on your 21st birthday. I'm surprised no one told you since those are rare, and they have a soulmate who is an angel. They are supposed to show you the way, and with their blood you can have angel powers along with witch ones."

I looked at him and told him, "Nope, no one told me any of that, and I have yet to have a soulmate since they don't exist."

He laughed, "Too bad my brother is a dumbass,

and you have so much potential with your fighting spirit. I just might have to have you for myself since you are a pretty thing."

He lunged at me, and I don't think I ran under the table to be in a place without him getting me. I'm tiny so I can fit under a table. The battle broke out, and I watched the cute guy battle with a flaming sword.

He handles himself well as the leader clashes with him. The clash of the swords and smell of burning flesh are prevalent in the air as the guys are fended off. A few minutes later the battle stops, and a cute guy is left standing with a few cuts on his arms but that is it.

The evil leader left, and is catching his breath, "We will be back for her Felix. Expect us we need her to escape from hell permanently.." They shimmer and disappear.

"What the hell just happened?" I asked confused.

I came out from under the table and looked at Ginger and Felix.

"Can you tell me what is going on finally?" I ask them wanting to know why those assholes tried to hurt me.

Ginger smiled at me, "You're special since you are a hybrid Angel Witch. Your mom was a powerful witch, and your dad was an archangel."

My eyes widen, "Is that why I have a stone that allows me to see them?" I asked.

She nodded and turned to face me full on. She

knew I needed to hear what she had to say, and it was going to take me a moment to allow it to sink in.

"Yes, but once you accept your full gifts then you will be able to see them naturally without help. I have been doing this for a while, and I'm part angel too. The guy next to me." She said pointing to the guy, "Is Felix one of your protectors, and your angel soulmate. Angel Witches are a special kind of witch that needs an Angel mate to come into their power. They complete you, and he will show you how to use the angel ones. I will show you how to use the witch ones. It's better than working retail killing your soul."

The world is now spinning. Wow! I just cannot believe it. The stones, the negative energy leaking off me when I shower. The people I can read, and influence even read their very thoughts. It makes sense now.

"What do I do now? How is this going to help me?"

"Well, the dark angels or lost souls came from a dark realm comparable to hell. They use people like you as slaves or kill you to steal your powers. So, we have to protect you at all costs."

"Thanks?" I tell them not really knowing what to do.

"The ritual will have to be performed so you can protect yourself. It will also give you the ability to heal faster." She told me.

Felix is silent then said, "Right then. I will be helping you access your angelic gifts and you'll be able to fly just like me." And he flexed his wings, and moved them lifting himself off the ground as though he was made of air.

"I can do it too?" I asked him not believing I can magically sprout wings.

He nodded, "When you receive your full powers I will teach you how to fly."

I smile thinking it will come in handy to get to work like that. Nope, then again I could not do it since I don't want that asshole Kyle getting any ideas. Kyle is a prick and letting him see it would not help at all.

"What about the dark Angels won't they be back?" I asked.

"They will but as I said I'm here to protect you." He smiled at me making my heart jump since he is a sexy, protective guy. It has been a long day since I'm winding down from the fight. I was happy to catch my breath.

"Thanks, and work?" I ask since I still need to make money even if it's a measly $8.90 an hour.

"You can go to the Luxor realm, and work there instead for more money. The Luxor realm is built for people like us."

"Luxor?" I asked with an eyebrow raised since I've never heard of the place before.

"A realm for supernatural creatures, or you can go to the Angelic realm called Super Celestial with the Angels. Of course, you have to be careful in not letting in the human souls. And be careful of the irritating Delco blobs you need a special gun to kill them." Felix explained.

"Wow...that will be cool."

"Of course, you do have to visit the Angelic realm to have your initiation there, and that's not an issue for witches with angel mates since they can teleport there."

"This is amazing I mean I have watched movies and television shows with Witches, but I never knew they actually existed."

"Yes, I was amazed too once I was allowed into the city. Of course, you have to go through special doors, so you won't be mistaken for a lost soul."

"Lost soul?"

"When humans die they come to the realm, and get in line with ID cards to be allowed into heaven or taken to a hell like place like a limbo of sorts, or even to hell itself called Blood Well where the dark angels are. The lost souls are used as slaves there, and even tortured."

"Interesting."

Ginger smiled, "Being a witch is fun too since Luxor has places to sell goods. They even let witches have free housing depending on where you go."

"I'm really happy to find this out after getting sick of dick Kyle and his bullshit." I tell Ginger finally admitting to me being sick of all the shit at the retail store where I work.

"I bet I know all too well what retail is like." I said.

"Wow..." I can't believe this is happening now of all times. On my day off too, and here I was planning to stay in and watching television the entire day. This is so much better than that. My emotions are buzzing all over the place.

"What do we do about the dark angel guys in the meantime? Does this mean Felix will be with me everywhere?" I asked imagining him going to places with me everywhere.

"I have to until you're strong enough to protect yourself. Of course, your guardian angel Kalisa is there with you too in the store to keep an eye on you and protect you."

My eyes widened, "Kalisa is my guardian angel? I have known her for a long time, and she never told me any of this?" I said wondering what else has been a lie.

I can't handle this, so I pace around the room. My heart races, and I think of all the times we hung around each other. I thought they were invisible, and I guess that's not the case. She never told me because it wasn't her job to yet.

"But how are you going to go out with wings visible to the world aren't they a dead giveaway?"

He straightened up his body, and his wings retracted and folded up against his body as if they were not there. Just like magic....

CHAPTER SIXTEEN

Watching them I knew that my own magic was somewhere deep inside me. It was glowing and I could feel it wanting to erupt. I'd felt this time and time again, but I never knew what it was. Now that I know I have to practice.

"There's a lot you still have to learn Angeline, but you'll get there. Why don't you give it a try and see if you can center your gravity enough to become one with your surroundings." Felix said.

"We can also turn invisible to the humans if we wish." In the blink of an eye, he is now gone. I just stood there in shock after everything stops spinning I will be good. Then my world will be full of not normal things, and it will be normal to me eventually. It's still all new to me.

"Amazing huh?" He asked me if I just nod still lost in thought.

"Yes, everything I have known is a lie. My friend

is really my guardian angel, and I'm a half angel witch that has gone so far down the rabbit hole that I'll need medication."

I take a deep breath letting it all sink in since I nearly lost my life. Thanks to me being a person who is not human at a dead-end job that makes you hate humanity anyway. I sat down and put my head down.

A hand rubs my back leaving me a warm fuzzy feeling like I'm floating on air. I loved the touch, and I looked up its Felix smiling at me. At least I have a cute guy in my life, and that's the one awesome thing. I have an angel soulmate.

"Thanks. I needed that I just can't believe I'm something else, and it does explain the powers."

Ginger stands in front of me, "We will protect you, and everything will be okay since you have Kalisa by your side."

I sigh, "I just hope I can protect myself soon since I'm really not the type to need a man for protection."

"I thought you were that type..." He said shocking me with how well he knew someone like me.

"I have been ever since I learned that I had to rely on me, and that was it."

"Yes, that will explain it."

"It does since I have known her long enough to know how independent she is." Ginger smiled at me knowing all too well that I don't need a man to protect me. I just wish I did not have to work for an asshole like Kyle...

I comply, "Okay, but just until I come to my full powers."

He nodded, "Of course, since you won't need me in that way after you get them."

I leave it at that since I got my point across. I get up deciding to face the music, and bask in the moment. My life is going to change, and it will be a welcome one since I will finally know who I am.

After that I ask them the next step, "When will the ceremony take place?"

"In a few days which means we need to gather ingredients for the ritual so you can accept your AngelWitch powers." Ginger said.

Just like that we are off. I follow wherever they are going next. Ginger gathered red, blue, green, yellow, and white candles. Next, is a black stick or that is what it looks like to me. Then we collected all we had at this shop. Then we got out of the store, and all of us piled up in a car.

Ginger drives, Felix is next to her in the passenger seat, and I'm in the back. I buckled up not wanting to go through the wind shield. We pulled out of the parking lot. Felix relaxed and his blue eyes stared ahead with the seat back.

"We need to make a stop in Luxor, and then take you to the Supercelestial realm too. It requires two stones an angel and a witch one that you have to take to find on your own. You will be tested to see if you have what it takes to be one if, so you receive a stone from each."

Wow...I'm a little scared since it takes a lot to prove you are worthy.

"Yes, the reason is because Angel Witches are a special breed. Half angel and half witch and they are rare to find since they can use angel and witch magic and even have their powers."

"Amazing. How many of them are left besides me?" I asked wanting to know how many more of us are out there.

"You're the only one that we know of here, and the rest are in Luxor and Super Celestial."

"Good to know that I'm not alone."

He smiled, "Yes it is. I have been tracking down you in particular for years. And the best thing is that we can date our charges, and some do couple up especially if they are Angel mates like we are. This is an unbreakable bond that will form between us once we have the ceremony. We will be able to read the others mind, and we are perfect for each other too." Felix said.

"Good to know since I've been looking for someone who will treat me right."

Interesting too since he is super sexy. At least I finally found out the missing piece to my heart.

"Would I be able to see my mom?" I asked wanting to find out the truth of why she gave me up.

Ginger smiled while concentrating on driving,

"That is where we are going to head to. Your mom is a high priestess, and helps people like you too."

I smile happy to have one more piece of the puzzle.

"Does that mean I can meet my father when we go to the Super Celestial realm?" I asked since he is the last piece of the puzzle.

"Yes, and they will explain to you why you had to go to the Crystal Crest realm. Don't worry you're not the only one that has to go there when they are growing up."

"Good to know it's not just me…"

I told him, and he is silent the rest of the way. The car stopped, and we got out of the car. We walked to a big door that shimmered in the wind, and Ginger waved her hand over it.

The door mechanism unlocked like it was a door handle. It opened and we stepped inside. I'm amazed at the sight.

Creatures of all kinds walk to and from the various shops. It was amazing to see since it was like they lived in their own world away from humans. Amazing too. We walked across the street, past shops, and we finally arrived at a huge, gated mansion. It was amazing. I loved the tall statues of gargoyles lining the entrance, and the closer we got the nervous I became.

Felix rubbed my shoulder to release some of the tension I've been feeling, "It's okay nothing bad will happen."

I smiled, "I know it's just too much at times, and I need a break."

"It is but you'll get used to it, and in time you will be fully adjusted to it."

"Plus, your mom wants to meet you since she made you stay at Crystal Crest until you can take the ceremony to receive your witch powers." Ginger said reassuring me, and she was silent walking there till now.

We made it to the front door of the mansion. Ginger knocked using the ornate knocker on the door. The door unlocked and all three of us got inside. I'm amazed about what I see.

The inside of the mansion looked like it had come out of a horror movie. The interior has red walls, and blue marbled flooring. I can tell I was in the living room since there is a fireplace, and chairs are placed in the corners. I loved the elaborate mansion already.

I followed Ginger and Felix down a hallway lined with pictures, and my nerves start going crazy. My heart starts hammering and my palms sweat because of the anticipation of meeting my mom. The closer we get the more excited I get about finally meeting her.

Once we got to the end of the hallway Ginger knocked on the door.

Knock...

Knock...

The door opened, and the woman behind it was very beautiful. Long flowing black hair, blue eyes like a waterfall, and pale translucent skin like me. Age made her skin flawless, and her eyes showed a wisdom in them that I have yet to have. She radiates energy off her like a sickly-sweet perfume.

She smiled at me when she met my eyes, "Angel, I'm glad you're doing well. I never would have imagined you to look this beautiful. I can tell that you're mine, and dads too."

I smiled at her, "Thanks…"

"What are you doing with your life now?" She asked the dreaded question people ask to find out what they are doing for the rest of their lives.

"Working at Kyle's General Store in Crystal Crest as a sales associate, and at this point I'm going to look for a new job since I'm an Angel Witch. I want to do more in my life then work a shitty retail job."

She smiled, "You should since you can work in Luxor or the Angelic realm now."

"Exactly." I told her seeing the light at the end of the tunnel. No more retail would be awesome. No asshole customers and no getting yelled at for stupid reasons by power hungry managers.

"You will, and you can make the witches and angels work together to stop the dark angels from killing us all."

"No pressure huh?" I told her.

"Only a little but for a good cause of stopping the bad guys."

"I can do it." I tell her fully capable of stopping

them. I will definitely do more with my life then just work retail because it's not for me at all.

She smiled at me, "You're my daughter of course you can. Take this." She said.

She opened up a cabinet near her desk, and took out a box. The box is wooden with witch symbols carved into it. She opened the box, and in it there was a white stone with flecks of color in it. Opal.

"This is a powerful stone that can make anything your mind wants to happen. It will happen in the blink of an eye." She explained.

I stare at it sitting there on the soft, red pillow. I touch it and the power course through me. The energy of it fills me like a cup of water to a person in the desert. I finally know what I have to do. I took it.

"This stone is especially for Angel Witches because of how powerful it is. Don't take it lightly because using power does not come without a price."

"No, it doesn't." I tell her fully knowing there is a price to pay for using it.

I have to do this though in order to become an Angel Witch. I have to do something more in my life then dealing with asshole customers.

I will pay the price of it because I have no choice. Not to mention dealing with Kyle for several years will get on your nerves for the longest time. He rode me by putting me on the front register when I hate it.

I really hate it, and he knows why he does it. He

is a jackass. I have a destiny now, and that's way better then working at a job that I hate.

I take the box with the stone, and then head to the Angelic realm with Felix along with Ginger we end up taking the car. The way to the realm is quiet and I see streets, restaurants, and towns pass by in a blur.

After sometime Ginger stopped the car and said, "Felix will take you from there since I can't go in with you. You'll have to do the Angel part of the ceremony there to get your wings and powers. We'll meet at my shop and do the witch part with your mom's help. I'll see you later."

Felix and I got out of the car. I was finally spending time with him alone. My soulmate. It's going to be fun to meet dad for the first time. I wonder if he approves of his daughter dating someone like Felix, and I know he is a badass with the sword.

We head to a fountain of a mermaid next to a door. He hit a button near the door.

"Felix here and I've got Angeline with me, and we need to see her dad Archangel Michael."

"No problem, we've been waiting to meet her once we heard she had been found."

A dark blue door appeared like magic with a mermaid knocker, and it rose up to let us enter the realm. I step inside and I'm amazed about what I see. It's pretty with creatures flying and walking to and from places.

There are angels everywhere flying to their houses. Some of the houses are in the air as if held by an invisible force. Dragons exist since they are flying around with creatures riding their backs. I follow Felix amidst the people.

We cross a few streets and pass by restaurants, shops, schools, and even an angel wing stations. We arrive at a place called The Skyline. I followed Felix inside, and it's a huge place with dragons flying in and out with creatures riding them without wings.

"The Skyline was created for creatures who need to get to the second level of the realm, but don't have wings to fly. They use dragons because the water serpents, and even ice dragons along with fire breathing ones are easier to tame and maintain."

I follow Felix deeper inside past creatures, and end up dock seven.

"This is the dock where royals use to get places. It's strictly reserved for only the elites to use. Elites are the archangels, and their families along with the other creatures that rule the Angelic realm."

He walked over to the keypad to the dock, and typed the code in. The doors opened and a blue scaled dragon with wings came out. It was amazing since I've never seen a dragon before. It had blue eyes like the endless ocean, and it looked like more than animal intelligence is behind it's gaze.

Felix smiled at me and my heart jumped. He is so unbelievably hot it's not even funny. I love finding out about this. Felix put a foot over the back of the dragon, and sat on the seat that is fastened to it like a horse stirrup. There is another one in front of it. It must be a two-seater.

He held out his hand, and I took it and swung my leg over. I put my feet in the stirrups, and he wrapped his arm around me while I held on for dear life.

"Take us to the Archangel's Palace." He told the dragon, and I had no idea they can understand him and speak English too.

The dragon kicked up his wings, and we are off to the Archangels palace. We fly through the air with the wind whipping our faces. I felt happy soaring in the air on a dragon.

CHAPTER SEVENTEEN

Riding on a dragon was exhilarating, and there were times when he went upside down that I thought I was going to fall off. I never fell off even when the dragon went upside down and right side up trying to avoid the other dragons that flew in its path.

It was the best experience I've ever had, and I loved riding it. It was better than riding a ride at Shadow World. Which is a spooky amusement park in Crystal Crest with rides, food, and awesome shows. I absolutely loved it, and I can't wait to learn how to fly at this point. At some point we finally land, and I get off the dragon.

We landed at the end of Dock eleven and I looked around at the unfamiliar landscape. It led directly to Michael's palace, so no extra walking was done to get to our final destination. Thank god cause I'd rather get it over with.

We get to the front door of the palace after we

get out of the dock. Two angel guards stood on both sides of the door, and one of them looked at us.

"Finally, they've arrived. Welcome home Angeline." Michael said.

I look at him with my eyebrow raised, "Uhh...thanks?"

The guard smiled back, "Don't be so shocked you have been a princess since your mom married dad. It's only natural that you will return home, and one day rule us."

"I can't even be a supervisor at a retail store let alone rule a realm. Don't call me one."

Felix looked at me, "Yes, you can even though you are half witch we need someone like you to bring the realms together to eliminate the dark angels issue. You will make a good ruler when you take over with me. I'll help you so don't worry you are not alone in this." He reassured me.

I loved him for it, and I met my match finally. I can do anything with him by my side.

"Welcome home."

The doors opened, and it led to a big room with a see-through glass floor, and it even had clouds underneath it. Don't look down though, and the top was a painted mural at the very top which was see through as well.

Felix took my hand, and we walked hand in hand to see Archangel Michael. There are chairs on a raised stage. They are white, and made of carved stone like a throne. Michael is in the middle. A woman was on his left and a child about my age was on the right. The woman straight up glared and the son my age looked at me confused. I had no idea what was going on either.

Michael met my eyes and smiled at me, "I can tell you are mine by the way you carry yourself. Welcome home Angeline. The woman on the left is Armory my ex-wife and the child is your half-brother Raiden. I never expected you would be this pretty, and I thank Felix for keeping you safe along with your guardian Kalisa. Felix will make a good king one day."

"You can't know that a half breed will be a great ruler, and your wife is a hot head that can't make logical decisions. Don't say that because for we know they could be our downfall." Armory said, and a part of me wanted to hit her for the half-breed comment.

"Or maybe you should shut up already. You cheated on me with your ex-boyfriend. Deal with the consequences already. I need to have a word with her alone anyway."

Michael got up and held out his hand, "Come with me, and I'll show you all you need to know in order to stop the dark angels."

I do as he said, and Felix came with me as we followed my father to talk leaving behind the crazy ex-wife and son. We walked with him up the stairs, and passed hallways till we got to the door. He took a key out of his pocket, and then opened the lock. We went inside, and it led to a big office/library combo. The library smelled like old books my favorite scent too. I inhaled it, and it was better than the finest perfume.

"This is my personal office, and I'd rather have a talk about this in private versus publicly in front of them. They do know about you, but they don't know about the dark angel situation. It can cause a straight up war if they were to find out about it. They need to be dealt with quietly. I'm married to your mom to keep the peace between the Angels and Witches since we need them to help us if something happens. Having you was a decision we made to bring them together, and to make them see eye to eye. My ex-wife doesn't like it because she wanted the throne to go to her son, but it might not happen if you decide to take it since me marrying you mom means it's you on the line. She doesn't like it, and tries to belittle me at every turn. She cares about herself more than the people."

Interesting at least I have Felix with me.

"I'll do my best to stop the bad angels who is the leader?"

"Zackary, my brother who was cast out of heaven for letting the demons escape from hell. I put him in the prison he is supposed to stay in for all eternity, and he got out due to times when the cage is down temporarily. He is trying to get you to escape from there permanently. We cannot allow that which is why once you become a half angel witch you have the power to permanently seal him in hell with my help." Felix told me.

"Good then let's do it." I tell them fully ready to accept that responsibility especially if it was with Felix. He is mine after all, and after hurricane Travis I needed someone better in my life. I need someone who will treat me right. I just want to move on with my life, and stop working for Kyle and retail in general. It's not for everyone either.

Michael smiled, "Good to see you have my spirit, and you will need something for the Angel Store here before you can do it."

Then he went behind his desk, and pulled out a red box. He opened it, and sitting on the pillow was a stone. A rainbow-colored stone that looked like waterfalls are rainbow colored. He brought it closer to me, and I could feel it calling to me.

"This stone is called Angel Fire, and it's what allows you to have your wings. It combines with the witch one to bless you with your powers." He gave it to me, and I put it in my purse for later.

"We already know what to get at the store: ambrosia, angel wing dust, and a few other things too right."

"Basically, don't forget sparkles in a jar, the special candles that they have to bring you into your power which will be found by using an associate there. If they know it's for you they will do their jobs, and not jerk you around. Especially if you are nice to them then they will definitely go above and beyond for you. Give them an attitude and they will give you one back."

I know that all too well since I tend to go out of my way for the nice people, and not so much for the mean people. They make everything suck, and I hate being on the other side.

"Will do, and I'll be a full AngelWitch in no time. I'll stop Zack with Felix's help, and we can go on to find more of them."

"Sounds like a plan now I know you are mine since you have a plan versus making one up. Enjoy getting the ingredients from there since most of the staff are actually friendly."

"Okay, I'll take your word for it. What am I going to pay with?"

"Felix can take my card since it's on me. Have fun and bring it back to me."

My dad gave Felix the card, and he put it in his wallet which had a picture of an angel holding a gold scepter straight in front of him. The background was metallic blue.

"We will and I'll make a list of what we need beforehand to take with me. I know my way around a retail store, and I'm pretty sure I can find it really quickly. Unlike the customers that walk-through Kyle's asshole store. I'm pretty sure that my brains will not leave me when I enter it."

I told him ready to be done with Kyle's once and for all.

Felix smiled at my dad, "Thanks, I'll take care of your daughter, and she will not leave my sight."

He laughed, "Good then after you get the ingredients we can do dinner and discuss the ritual. I do want to be there when it happens since I need to have people witness it. Then you will be given a tattoo and marked as an elite with the ability to go wherever."

"Thanks, and we will discuss it after we get the ingredients. I want to see the book to know how the ritual will go."

"Okay, and now we can see the book and make a list."

Michael went behind his desk, and pulled something behind it. The bookcase shuttered, and opened up leading to a room.

"Come with me."

We followed him, and I went past the desk to the room. It led to a lit hallway with pictures of angels on the wall minus the halo.

"What no halos?" I asked Felix.

"Nope, that's a myth people make up and it's only for ones in heaven. Or lost souls. This is not the heaven for human souls since they go through a checkpoint. They are given an ID which is checked at the Gate, and they go through one if they are good, or the other if they are bad."

"Interesting..." I told him.

The room the hallway led to an even bigger room which had all kinds of ritual items in it. There was a stand and on it sat a cerulean book. The Angel Ritual Book I assume. The room had all kinds of items in it such as: candles, herbs, stones, and everything else you would need for rituals. I love the place and there are even pictures of the various archangels all over the room. It felt more like home then my apartment did. Michael walked up to the stand, and opened the book flipping through the pages until he found the one he was looking for.

"Found it come here both of you." He said proudly.

I go up to where he is and browse over the ritual. I look over the ingredients. I got out a pen and a mini notebook, one of the ones I have for work. I write everything down in a journal to record my experiences. I take the time to write down my tasks for the day, and anything else I will remember too.

List:
Ambrosia
Angel Wing Glitter
Special Wing Shirt (It allows the wings to pop through)
Blue and white candles
Essence of arch angel

"Interesting, but what is essence of arch angel?" I asked him hoping it did not involve killing in the ritual to get said item.

"Energy from a past angel. It's rare, but they have it at Silver's in the special items section."

"This will be the first time I've seen it since they did not give me an AngelWitch mate till now." Felix said he didn't believe it either.

It's unreal to be even talking about it at times. I felt his disbelief as if it were my own.

"Yes, it's strange but it's the way someone is given power from the Angels. It transforms your entire system, and even your body will be like an angels. No sickness, no aging, and it will be different since you are part witch." He replied.

"I'll keep that in mind. What time does the store close?"

"It closes at 10, so plenty of time to shop and get everything we need."

"Good let's go." Felix said. Before we left dad gave us a phone for us to use in the realm, and then he programmed in his number in. It was a cool touch phone, and it listed the weather which is 70 degrees. Nice and best of all it was a metallic blue too.

"This will allow you to stay connected with me period since it can be used to talk to me in between realms. Just press a number for Luxor, Crystal Crest, and the Angel Realm." He said, and I put it in my pocket.

I even programmed Felix's number too, and it's going to be neat to finally talk in between realms. Although a part of me is not ready to go back to a store, but an angel store is different? I hope so since the angels had to be smarter than the human customers.

"Where is the Angel Store?" I asked him.

"On the lower level of the realm. I've been there to ward off a crazy ex and to pick up some ingredients for it. They can even do the ritual for you."

"Are we taking the dragon?"

"Yes, and then we can text your dad when we are done."

It's good to have a phone like this since it means I don't need to worry about going to the fitting room to page a person, and it's not like they would be able to anyway. They can't use it unless it's an emergency well Kyle's doesn't. Some locations do. I never liked asking sales associates for help since I could do it myself.

We make it to the bay and take the dragon to the lower levels where the shops are. The dragon ride down is amazing as well as the sights to see. People and creatures flying everywhere. I bet it's way different to shop there then at Kyle's.

We get a car to drive the rest of the way to the store. I'll have to ride in the car till I get my wings, and then I can fly instead. The realm is busy on the drive there with angels going to and from places. Restaurants, gas stations, shops, schools, hospitals, and other places whiz by. It was a cool place, and once I get used to everything it will be a good place to call home.

"I love the apartments here, and we can live here to if you want." Felix told me, and I will definitely think about it. It would mean breaking the lease I have, and packing up everything and moving to a different place.

"And colleges?" I asked.

"You can go to Angelite University to study whatever you want to major in whether it is English,

History, and whatever else you wish to study. They even have a military and a ton of other places to explore." He told me as we waited in traffic.

Traffic can suck here like it does in the Crystal Crest realm. After ten minutes we hit a traffic light, and pulled into a parking lot with various shops and stores. Right at the center of it is a huge building with revolving doors, and a big sign called Silver's Angelic Emporium.

CHAPTER EIGHTEEN

We have arrived at our destination. The place is all decked in dark blue, and we park the car. The place is already busy with people going in and out of the store with people pushing carts.

It was a bustling store, and I really hope to get in and out fast. I love finding items and sometimes when it comes to shopping. I do hate the crowds. Luckily, it is a weekday so not that bad. Not like a weekend after the holidays. I do enjoy seeing the way new stores do things.

We get further inside, and I see that the carts are glitter blue, and the handle is a light glitter blue. It's pretty in the realm and sunny too. A better environment then Kyle's since half of the customers are miserable pieces of shit.

I feel like here I will finally be able to escape it all. That's a good thing for me. Finding out I was an angel witch is the best thing that could happen to me.

I will never have to deal with the miserableness of Kyle's general store again.

I even grabbed a map of the store since they have them right in the front. Handy and we end up grabbing a small, handheld cart since we are not doing a lot of shopping at all. I look at the list, and the place it busy with activity.

Some of the customers are not even in a bad mood at all. They are actually nice. The aisles are big enough to not worry about bumping into someone. Items are on display for the seasons, and placed strategically throughout the store.

It's a really cool place, and better then the retail store I work at. The employees seem like they love their job instead of hating it like the ones at Kyle's. The registers are in the front, and they are all smiling too.

Every single register is lit and none are empty. The lines aren't long like in Kyle's either. With a map in hand, I look for all the ingredients in the list. I even mapped it out and I hope they have everything in stock. I already have a cart I make my way to the women's section which is the closest to pick up the shirt.

I find the shirt easily since they have a whole section dedicated to those shirts. I look through them and look for my size which is a medium in my favorite color. They even have it in black with silver glitter.

I pick out a few more for later since it's not on my tab.

Felix smiled at me, "Very you. I figured you would love those shirts."

"Yes, and I love shopping if I'm not on the other end. It's a different story when I'm not working."

I take the shirts and put them in the basket. I take them off the hangers, and leave them there so other people can use them. I don't take hangers with me since they can use them for other customers clothes.

I take my time and look at all the cool brands they have. The shirts alone are $5.00 each. Not too bad. I get done in those sections and head over to the ritual section.

I found it easily by looking for the sign. I get asked enough at work where everything is, and I can find it myself instead of asking a sales associate for it since I'm not a lazy asshole.

"You weren't lying when you said you know your way around a store..." Felix said smiling at me.

"Because I know how to find my way around after working at one for so long. I also hate people more then I used to because of it. I didn't enjoy working for Kyle since he was a douchebag. I'll be happy when I leave for good."

"I bet. I can't imagine dealing with the general public like you do. I've been a warrior all my life, so I really don't need to work retail since this is my job. I'm part of the Angel military so I get paid monthly

$2,000 every two weeks. I even get a free apartment there."

"That is good to know. I can use my abilities for good and help witches like me." I told him.

I can definitely see a future with him, and hopefully I can so something besides working retail. I hate the customers that come through Kyle's since they yell at you over things you can't control. Don't get me started on the supervisors since half of them don't know how to do their jobs.

I hate it one even made sure I went to the zone by asking my coworker if I went even going as far as getting another supervisor to keep track of me. There is a reason I'm leaving it all behind me.

I searched the aisles to find the angel wing glitter and the candles. All the various sections had places where you can check out there instead. Some were empty and in the back of my mind I scanned the room on the lookout for Zack.

I loved having Felix with me since he was added protection. It was nice having him around me, and I could see myself with him for a long time.

"Excuse me do you work here? I've been waiting for someone to assist me for 20 minutes. I need something out of the case, and they keep telling me someone will be with me…" An angel told me looking at me like it was my fault she was waiting.

"I don't work here. This is not even the same uniform, and it's regular clothes." I told her not to deal with her rude attitude on my day off.

"Well, you look like you do. Rude, stupid, and always ignoring me." She replied while glaring at me.

"I really hope they never assist you at all since I would hate to be the employee dealing with you." I told her then I left.

I can't believe the stupidity of some people...

"She actually thought you work here?" Felix asked not believing it like I did...

"Yes, she thought I did because I have an I work retail vibe. It happens..."

People are stupid when it comes to stores. I'm not even wearing the right uniform...I look for the items I need and grab the angel wing glitter and a few candles.

"See? She did not assist me and was very rude to me you should fire her!" The obnoxious angel said.

She managed to get someone to assist her all right as manager. Then accused me of working here and giving her bad service...Reminds me of the idiots at Kyle's. The manager even gives me and are you mental look.

"I don't blame her since she does not work here. She does not have to assist you if she is a customer, and she is Michaels stepdaughter so I would be careful if I were you. You don't want to get on his bad side trust me...."

The lady looked at him like he was crazy, "Good then I'll go to corporate over this..."

I mess with her because I was sick of her mouth. "Okay, I can't wait to tell Michael about this since I don't work here, and I don't have to assist you. I can't wait to tell my dad about this..." I said not even caring if I gave her a bitchy attitude.

I walked away after that. The nerves of some people. Now I had to get the rest of the items, and to quit retail once and for all. Felix laughed, and all I have to do is get the ambrosia and angel essence. It's been a fun experience. We head to the area where the ambrosia is and then all we have to do is get the essence.

"I know where they keep the last ingredient, and it's in a room for elites and their Protectors. Follow me." Felix told me and I followed him. We weaved in and out of the aisles passing by shoppers full of items. Angels are browsing items and examining them for flaws to see if they want to buy them. It was interesting to see all the different areas and some aisles are in the air. There are more levels then at Kyle's. Yes, it's a store, but it did not have a horrible feeling to it that Kyle's did. Most of the shoppers gave off good emotions. Emotions I can feed off and not feel drained. I can look them in the eyes without wanting to turn away. I don't even have to worry about not looking at their eyes. Nothing miserable or sad. No anger either, or yes there was the crazy lady but that is it.

We finally get to a door, and it's marked Specialty items. Felix pulls out a key card and ran it through the reader on the door. It opened and we stepped inside. Items lined the walls, and they were odd.

Animal parts, human parts, vampire fangs and blood, even werewolf and fairy blood. Then we get to an item on a stand surrounded by a glass case. Archangel essence. There is a guy behind the counter, and he smiled at me. He wore the uniform which is a dark blue shirt and black jeans. So not the uniform....

"So, you are Angeline huh? I'm Dariel the angel of Vampires. Weird, I know, but even vampires have angels to call on." Then he showed me a mouth full of fangs, and I smiled back at him.

"Nice to meet you. That's the last item I need for my ritual isn't it?" I asked him.

"Yes, and then we are done."

Dariel was cute too since he is tan with his dark hair pulled back in a ponytail. He has piercing brown eyes too. Damn. He felt like a warm blanket in my head unlike Felix. Felix felt like a warm fuzzy pair of slippers on a cold winter morning. He is a dream since he feels like safety. Time stops when I'm in his arms it's the best feeling in the world. Soulmates come around once and a while, and I've found mine which means I don't have to date cheating assholes anymore. I don't have to worry about being someone's side chick, and no worrying about if he calls me. What if he doesn't? I was sick of it all. I've been done with it ever since my ex cheated on me with one of my friends. I hated it and it made me question some of the partners I've had after him. It's a headache. I've been sick and tired of the dating world and men treating women badly. Forget it.

Dariel said, "Okay, then if you are all done shopping I can ring it all up here for you, so you don't have to wait in line?"

"Good since I hate waiting." Felix said and he is just as impatient as I am. He took the last item out of the case, and put it in a box. I handed him the rest of the items, and scanned them all. The total is $20.00. Felix gave him the card, and he ran it through. Everything is bagged so we left.

I was glad to get out of there since they are just as crazy as Kyle's even though they are better in some ways. Retail is crazy no matter what store, and I was ready to leave it all behind me. We head back to the car, and make it to my dad in time. We hurry to his place, and take the items inside. I text him the details about being on the way there. I never would have thought I would have a way of escaping that place. Kyle treats his employees like bodies not people. He punishes them, and fires them on a whim. You can bet your ass something will be done about it before I leave.

I need to for the employees sake. Especially Jasmine and her lazy ass supervisor. That bitch loads her up with freight and does not even bother to help out. She hates customers and wont serve them. Hell. She said she would take care of her price changes and forget it. She doesn't do her job, and seeing her fired would be awesome. She was supposed to take care of a ring that got lost in the mail five months ago and I doubt she would do it. Jasmine was supposed to be the supervisor, but bitchy Sandra got promoted instead because of the fact that dumbass assistant Laurie favored her instead. It's bullshit and I'll need to right that before I leave. It's about time I used the powers for good...

We got to the main room, and Felix is by my side as usual. My life was just me waiting until my actual life began. I love this new future.

Michael spotted us as soon as we got into the main room. Armory and Raiden were on both sides. I ignored it all.

"We have everything we need for the angel part, and all that's left is to perform the ritual to waken my powers." I told him.

"Good then we can discuss the ritual over dinner. I'm sure Armory won't mind watching the place when I'm gone." Then he got up and walked up to us.

"Yes, sir it would be an honor to join you for dinner." Felix said in a respectful manner.

"Definitely. We have much to discuss." Then we walked with him and ended up getting out of the palace to a limo waiting for us outside. A butler was holding the door open for us. I hopped in and then Michael went in followed by Felix who sat on the side he could see outside with.

I'm still not out of danger yet. I put on my seatbelt and Felix and Michael didn't.

Michael smiled, "Galen take us to Castiel's Bistro." He told the driver.

"Aye...Aye boss." the guy in front said.

Felix smiled, "Nice choice, since I love their food, and it's the prefect date night place too."

"Exactly, the perfect place to talk about the ritual and catch up." Michael said.

I was eager to spend more time with my father. I was entering a new world, and I wanted to know more about it.

"Good. If they have spaghetti and clams that sounds like heaven along with Dark Horse energy drinks. I love that combo."

Felix smiled, "That sounds good and thank god angels can eat. I don't want to give up food at all."

Michael smiled, "I'm happy about that too. Food is something I never want to give up."

The ride there was fun since we talked about everything. It was fun to talk to him, and put everything to the side for now. I was no longer an Angel Witch at that moment just a girl talking to a father she did not know. Castiel's Bistro was busy tonight, and the main sign had red lettering with a black background and border on it. I loved it since it reminded me of a fancy, expensive restaurant like the one in Crystal Crest that I go to for special occasions. It's set in an old house built in the 1800's I love it.

I love going to eat at new places since it lets me forget about my stupid retail job. Angels crowd the parking lot, and they are even dressed in nice attire. I felt like I was underdressed, but at the same time I did fit in. We get out of the limo and head inside. The decor is all red and black too. Black tables and chairs, red walls, and floors. A host stood in front of a computer, and it was a woman with long black hair and grey eyes. Her name is Lana. She looked up from her seating chart and spotted Michael. "How many people are we seating your royal highness?" She asked him since he has been here more times before.

"Table for three. Get me a private booth in the corner of the room."

She smiled, "Okay, then we have just the room. Follow me."

We followed her and she led us to a table in the corner. Angels sat at tables at various spots, and some of their wings are out while some are hidden. Servers carried food to and from tables, and giving them drinks. It was busy tonight and when they saw our party they took a second look. Probably because of Michael being there. I can see why since he is pretty good looking. He looks like a model and has the body to match. It was pretty cool to have a dad that ruled everything. I'm going to love my new life too. I wondered how the store was doing, and how Kalisa is. I wonder what will happen once I come into my powers. Does that mean I'll get closer to Kalisa? I've known her for so long, and now that I know about her true identity it makes me admire her more. I was not angry about her keeping a secret from me since I know she did it to protect me.

I sat across from Micael and Felix sat next to me. The host handed us menus, and I looked at it noticing all the various entrees, sides, and drinks.

They have sandwiches, burgers, and salads. I love this place, and it even had my favorite dish spaghetti and clams. Good, and I even see my favorite energy drink mixed with alcohol.

"Hi, my name is Christy. I will be your server. What can I get you to drink?" She asked and she was wearing a nice uniform too. Her wings are displayed for all the world to see just like her boobs. Even her eye makeup is done like her eyes are painted green and blue. She wore an almost slutty housekeeper outfit. She looked at Michael first. "I'll have a glass of Kano."

She smiled, "Good choice since we have the best in town. And you?" She asked me.

"A Dark Horse."

"Good choice as well, and lastly?" She looked at Felix.

"A Sparkling Volcano."

"Ooh…that's a popular one. I'll be right back with the drinks." Then she left to get the drink order.

I looked over the food and deciding what I wanted to eat. I saw a pasta dish that looked good, so I chose that since it had macaroni noodles, tomato, and clams. Yum. Michael and Felix browsed the menu to look for what they wanted to eat. There is silverware already placed on the table, and empty glasses too. A piano is playing classical music in the background giving it a nice atmosphere. I loved it since it's nice and looked like a fancy place with a nice feel to it. The server came back, and put our drinks down in front of us. They even brought bread and butter to eat while we waited for our food.

"Did you decide on what you wanted for food?" she asked concern in her eyes, and she looked at me first.

"I'll take a macaroni and clams with a side salad."

"What kind of dressing?"

"Ranch."

"Okay, and anything else?"

"Nope, that will be it for me."

"And what can I get you your highness?" she asked Michael.

"The steak and fries, medium rare, with the special Castiel's sauce. That'll be it."

"Okay, and you?" she asked batting her eyes at Felix. It made me want to hit her, but I didn't.

"Castiel's Big Ass Burger and fries. Well, done."

"Okay, no problem coming right up." Then she left to put our order in, and it left us plenty of time to talk. Even though I was hungry I still wanted to talk about the ritual and the Zack situation.

It was silent at the table for a few minutes, and Michael then decided to break the ice, "There is the ritual that needs to be done, and then the matter of dealing with Zack. He is trying to get a way back here, and to cause chaos in the realm. The only thing that can help with that is to perform a ritual opening the dimension between their realm and ours. It requires yours and Felix's blood. Even if you turn into an AngelWitch he can still use you it will just be stronger. The only way he can't hurt you is if you kill him."

"Okay, news to me I'll make sure he won't hurt her." Felix said very protective of me.

"Good just what I wanted to hear since he needs to be stopped, and that means you need to work together since you will be a team. I know it's a lot to take in, and when I married your mother I wasn't sure how it would turn out."

I smiled, "It was overwhelming at first, but I can handle it as long as I have Felix by my side."

"Good to know. There is something else I want to tell you as well. Armory is my ex-wife, and we had a child together. I hated the way she acted about it after we split. After we divorced I'm forced to help her by paying child support, and I hate the fact that she had him just so she could punish me for rejecting her. She hates the fact that I got involved with a witch. It's also even more insulting that I had you with her. To her, me marrying your mom was a slap in the face. She tried to make me cut ties with Raiden, but I can't. I want to be in his life. The reason I'm telling you this is because she will try to get in the way. Don't let her chase you away from me. I want to get to know you more, and if she does anything to you, I will be forced to kill her. I used to think I knew her until she tried to turn some of my subjects away from me."

My eyes widen, "She is horrible for trying to do that to you. You don't deserve to be punished because things didn't work out between you two. Divorces can get nasty like when my adopted mom was left by my dad thanks to his secretary, and he never used me once since it had nothing to do with me and everything to do with them. Children should not be used as pawns by the parents."

He smiled, "Thanks, I wish it were different, and I had to keep it a secret at first or else she will use it against me and not let me spend time with my son. I care about him, and he is half me after all. I just fell for the wrong person who doesn't take rejection well."

I smiled, "I can relate to that. Try breaking it off with someone who won't leave you alone even when you end things. I didn't want to hear about him and his exes either. He tried to harass me because of it, and finally I had to tell him to leave me alone, or I'll get a restraining order."

Felix's eyes widen, "Wow...good to know and if he ever comes back I will kill him for you and serve you his head on a silver platter..."

"Good. I can take him on though after I change into an AngelWitch since he is a human."

"I like to hear that my daughter can take care of herself, and it's better than my ex-wife who expects everyone to take care of her. "Michael said.

I was just happy to have my life going in the right direction. I'm sick of retail, and I hope to get out of it soon. All these new changes mean a new start…

I smiled, "Yes, I can. I'm also ready to stop Zack

and get the hell out of retail. It's boring doing the same thing day after day with no hope of making a difference or getting a promotion."

Michael smiled, "I worked at a retail store during my time that I went to college. I know how it is. They overwork you to the point where you no longer give two shits about the job. They should at least pay you more than they do. In the Crystal Crest realm, its minimum wage, and not $15 an hour like here. I raised the pay because they deserved to be paid more than they do. The stuff they have to deal with is amazing. Angry customers, dumbs managers who don't know what they are doing, and they get yelled at over stuff they have no control over."

"I'm constantly overworked by Kyle the evil store manager and his bitchy assistant does not help either. Yelling at me to do things when we are so short-handed and I'm running different departments. Me having to fight the customers service manager to not get on the register since a few people have to have breaks, and I'm watching phones and another service area. Being cross trained in different departments when there is no one there to cover it. It sucks. I thought I'd be stuck where I am till college, and it's a different story now. I'd take finding more like me and stopping Zack over retail any day."

"I bet and if there is anyone who stands in the middle of stopping Zack then take them out too." Michael said.

"We will and I'll make sure of it since I'm never

leaving her side at all. It's my job to protect her after all." Felix said a fierce look in his eyes.

"Good. Then we have nothing to worry about since everything will go as planned." Said Michael.

I took a sip of the drink, and it gave me the much-needed energy. I can sense feelings and influence them. The Angels around me are like balls of happy energy. Michael is the strongest of them all. Happy with a little bit of caution. Felix is happy, and I'd be happy too since it means a chance to be happy finally. I finally wonder what it will be like to feel magic at my fingertips. I would be able to have powers even more then now.

"What will I be able to do once I get my abilities? I can sense feelings, manipulate them, and even erase their memories." I told them.

Michael's eyes widen, "You should not be able to do that unless you are very powerful, or a leader."

Great. I'm more different in their world too.

"The only person capable of doing that is the leader of a coven, and I knew there was a leader in one of the AngelWitches somewhere. I didn't think I'd find her for a while. Together we can lead other witches and train them to be good." Felix said.

Me leader? I'd never want to be a supervisor at Kyle's. Too much ass kissing and ass riding.

Michael smiled, "Should have known me and your mom getting together having a child would be a special one. With this information we can have angels and witches on the same side with their offspring."

"That will be amazing to see them work together." Felix said.

"Yes, it will, and the vampires and werewolves will steer clear and not start stuff."

"Nope, we will not have to worry at that point."

I wondered how long this went on. I've stumbled into something bigger than me. Very big if what they are saying is true.

The server came over and she brought us our food. She put a bowl in front of me, and I dug in totally starving at this point. The side salad was even in a cute little bowl with a cup of my favorite dressing. I slathered it on, and took a bite. I loved to eat salads, and everything is fresh on it like it came straight out of the garden. Even the pasta and clams are tender. It was the best meal I've had in a while since I didn't cook much for myself. A lot of fast food is on my diet. I don't have the money to splurge. Not until I graduate college. That will be in a few years. I'll turn twenty-one soon and then I'll be legal to drink. The more I get away from this place and Crystal Crest the further away I'll be from my ex- Austin. I was sick of being treated like a side chick, and he never introduced me to his parents. He kept things from me, and he always bragged about deleting his messages of mine after he read them. A guy who had a bad history, and I was stupid to fall for his lies. I ended it after he tried to sleep with my friend. He took it badly, and I don't know why since he had someone else. He texted me things like, "My other exes regretted dumping me. Thanks for backstabbing me the way my other exes did. Thanks for killing me." The jackass was trying to make me feel guilty by saying he did all the things I wanted him to do.

I shivered and looked around the room.

"Are you okay? Are you cold?" Felix asked concern in his eyes.

"Yes, just thinking about some of the things I'll leave behind."

"Did you want to talk about it?" He asked.

I wanted to go into detail and tell him, but I wasn't ready yet. I didn't want Michael to know either.

"Maybe I'll go into detail about my crazy ex story, but I just want to focus on the task at hand."

"Fair enough."

I continue to eat, and make sure to hide it better. The last thing I need is to get distracted by an asshole. I don't want to think about it right now. No remembering stalking asshole. He was causing too much crap in my life. We had to always hangout in hotels like I was a dirty secret, and someone he did not want to bring home. He didn't want to talk on the phone, and all we did was text that's it. I didn't even care about the fact that he had a record since I was so in love with him. I wanted to marry him and him to move in with me. All of it came crashing down especially when he cheated on me with a friend. I caught them red handed in her bed. He was only making her think he was in love with her to get close to me. Liar...Liar pants on fire. He only wanted to use me for my place because he hated his mother, and would not have money because of it. Everyone saw it except me since in my own world he was perfect. Short black hair, brown eyes, tans, and a model for a magazine. We met at my job, and I was down after yet another failed relationship that almost resulted in marriage. He chatted me up and we started dating. 6 months of my life wasted with the wrong person. It hurt letting him go, but if he didn't make me happy I would have to leave him. Then he acted like he was the wounded party when he was the one that fucked up the entire time. Fuck him, and only once and he wasn't even good at it.

"Angeline?" Michael asked. I sucked at hiding my thoughts.

I looked at him, "Huh?"

"As soon as you come into your power your life will never be the same again."

"Oh, I'm so ready for a new start away from my shitty retail job, horrible ex-boyfriend, and shithead Kyle." I tell them not even thinking and just blurting it all out.

Felix's eyes wide and Michael just sat there mouth wide.

"Well, you don't have to worry about him anymore. He can't follow you here, and if he tries to hurt you I'll personally see him dead." He told me and I believed him.

"No one messes with my daughter and if he ever tries to touch you he is dead." Michael said.

I was definitely ready to be an AngelWitch. I needed it since I want a purpose to my life. I want to help others like me.

I can finally be with someone who cares about me. Felix smiled at me. He is all I needed at this point. I don't need anyone else.

"I can totally relate to you Michael and Angeline with the crazy ex part since mine tried to get me for money for someone who wasn't even mine. Just because I was a member of the Protectors, and it would mean she would get some of my money to support her lifestyle. Thanks to Angeline I'm free of her. If I take the bond to Angeline it negates the one I had with my ex which is a good thing."

I smiled at him, "I'm happy I could help with that since I know what it means to have a crazy ex. Mine was stalking me because I needed to be with someone who will treat me right. I don't want to be with someone who will keep me hidden like a dirty secret."

Felix smiled, "You shouldn't be kept a secret since you are so pretty to me. I'd be glad to have you on my arms."

I smiled at him because it was very sweet of him to say that.

Very sweet since it was something I needed to hear. I no longer felt the hurt my asshole ex caused. Instead, I felt something else like belonging to someone. I had to hide more than my personality, and I never got to know him at all. It was just texting and not talking.

"It'll be okay once you get away." Felix told me noticing my shaking hands. I can't help it since it makes me see red at times. Felix being by my side ensures that no one will hurt me. I shouldn't even be working retail because it can get so bad that I don't want to go in and getting assaulted by their energy fields. Just going into the place is draining enough.

"When you come into your powers you'll be able to control everything more, and human emotions won't bother you as much. I understand how hard it can be on an untrained angel, and especially one who is half witch. It'll be easier on you." Michael told me.

I calmed down some, and then said, "I'll be okay it's just an adjustment."

"Yes, you will because I'm not letting anything happen to you." Felix told me. I believed him, and I continued eating my food. I wanted to finish it all to keep things off my mind. Michael and Felix finished theirs and I was just ready at this point. After we got done Michael paid the bill and we left.

We headed to the palace and the limo ride was quiet for a few minutes.

"Time to perform the ritual, and it will be in the area where the book is." Felix said.

My palms were a little shaky, but it was my adrenaline rush kicking in. I can finally get my wings.

I hope I can handle my new responsibilities. I

hold the bag with all the ritual items. My life is going to be different. Thank god I have some days off.

"I thought I had to do it on my 21st birthday?" I told Michael.

"You can do it on it or near it. It really doesn't matter." he told me.

Of course, it also meant tying myself to Felix and that things would change. I won't have to worry about dating either.

"Okay, then let's do it." I told them to be ready to take on the powers. I go up to the book, and put down the items in the center of the table. There was enough room on the table to put the items needed.

Michael went up to the center of the stand. I moved out of the way.

"Stop right there." a voice said, and I looked to see where it was coming from Armory. A look of hatred on her face directed to Michael.

"No, you can't stop it this time I won't let you..."

"Yes, you will because I have every reason to kill her since she is an abomination. One I can't allow to exist." she said like all psychos do. God, this is going to be a fun day.

"Not on my watch. Felix took her and the items with the book. Do it without me and I'll take care of Armory..."

I grabbed the bag, and Felix took the book and put it in the bag. We ran away from the scene.

"Don't worry I know where to take you follow me." Felix said saving the day.

I followed Felix and we had to find another base. The ritual had to be completed.

"That's not the only place we can go to in order to escape from Armory."

A part of me hoped Michael killed her since she was a pain in the ass. We made it back to the dragon bay. We chose his dragon and hop on him.

"So, is it still in this realm?" I asked him.

"Yes, a very secret part of it. You remember when we said there were more of you?" he told me. I nodded.

"We built a place secretly for you all to hide. We knew people wanted to get you AngelWitches, which is why we built a secret island for training. The leader of the island is an AngelWitch herself with an Angel-mate to help her run it."

I look at the cell phone while on the dragon, and there is also a number from my mom's cell. I texted her.

Armory interrupted the ceremony, and Felix is taking me to the island.

I hit sent.

I got a ring back a few minutes later.

Okay, I'll be there since I need to talk to you anyway.

*No problem...*sent.

I just enjoy the rest of the time after that. I hold Felix tight and happy to at least have him in my life. After Austin I thought the dating world would suck, but with Felix things might be different. I feel safe and solid in his arms. It makes me happy knowing I have someone on my side. Someone to be there for me and catch me when I fall. I felt like I was never able to open up to Austin as much as I have to Felix. I'm looking forward to getting to know him more, and we do need to spend time together especially since we are going to be stuck together for a while.

It can be a good thing to have someone there for you for a very long time.

"Almost there." Felix told me, and I looked over his shoulder and there was an island surrounded by water. It was all pretty lush and green. I could feel the magic coming off it. It's really welcoming to me and now I finally feel like I've come home.

"It recognized you doesn't it?" he asked me.

I nod, "Yes, and it's like I finally know where I belong."

I told him. I feel good like nothing will hurt me. Then something whirs by my head....

...A fire ball that tried to block the dragon. Felix knew exactly how to avoid it. He guided the dragon out of harm, and I looked behind me. It was Zack and he was riding on a black-scale dragon.

Next to him was Austin. My heart drops and my anger takes over. A force I've never felt roars through me, and I have no idea where to direct it to. I hold out my hand and take all the anger I feel then throw it at Austin. It hit him like an energy ball and made him fly back. He fell off the dragon he rode, and I laughed as he fell to his death. The blast destroyed the dragon too, and I actually felt bad about that.

Zack's eyes widened and he retreated…Take that asshole.

"Damn, I've never seen that from you before. Who was he?" Felix asked me with curiosity.

"Austin the crazy ex…He had it coming too." I told him.

"He deserved it, and I'm not surprised. If Zack is after someone he usually lets the person's ex on it for fun. After he takes a person's power they are useless to him…just toys." Felix shivered.

I really don't want to think about why he did… Probably…horrifying.

Felix got really close to the island, and the space above him was humming like it was alive with energy. He waved his hand, and it ripples and parts away to let us through. The dragon dives down through the space and it closes above us. We dived down and after a few minutes the dragon landed on the grassy ground.

I got off first and Felix helped me down. The dragon shimmers and changes into a person. A guy with a long, braided, ponytail, brown eyes that drew you in with tan skin and a fit body. He had on black jeans and boots. He winked at me, "Well, that was more excitement then I thought. They usually don't chase us unless they want someone very important. Who are you?" He asked me curiosity plain in his eyes.

"Angeline Mystica."

His eyes widen, "Then it's a good thing we have

met. My name is Nick Spaine. I'm a dragon shifter King sent to guard AngelWitches. This is my island called Haven. I call it that since it's a safe place for AngelWitches to go to. I knew Felix was your Protector. I wanted to escort you myself. I'm his dragon in battle, and you will have one to help you too. One will be assigned to help guard you and help you in battle."

"That will be good to have."

Nick laughed, "Yes, I love being around them too. We can even heal with their abilities, and some people can even get attached to them to the point where they can be lovers if they choose. Girl angel witches and guy dragons or guy ones and girl dragons."

"Okay..." I say wondering what it felt like at the same time weirded out by it. Nick is sexy, but Felix is my Angel Mate, and I don't want to mess it up.

"I doubt she would want to even though you are my dragon to call on. I don't like sharing..." Felix told him.

"Some do..." Nick teased back...

Felix just glares at him.

"Now let's go inside and I can show you around the place..." Nick said, and he walked toward the building facing us. It was a huge, gothic style mansion straight out of a movie. It was huge with a black wallet outside and the celling was black too. It was a fun looking place too. The door is wooden with an angel wing knob.

AngelWitches and Angels are all over the place, and it was prominent in the living room as soon as Nick opened the door. Busy with AngelWitches and there are even dragon statues throughout the place. It was all black and red furniture and pictures of angels and dragons all over the place. I loved the feel of it, and they were very welcoming and saying hi to me.

"People love the fact that you are here, and now we can stop Zack." Nick said.

Hearing that warmed my heart. I hope I can save them from Zack. I hoped my ex died cause the last thing I need is an asshole alive.

"This mansion was built to house future Angel-Witches, and it's big. It has a huge library, a big computer space with a ton of computers. A commercial kitchen, ten or more bathrooms, sixty bedrooms. A training room for magic and spells. A huge ritual room, a gym, and several living rooms and even a ballroom for events."

"Nice place. My mom said she would meet us here." I told him.

"She arrived a few minutes ago, and is waiting for you in the ritual area. You need to become an Angel-Witch. We have to do it today and it will stop Zack from trying to steal your powers. It's easier before the ritual." Said Nick.

"Okay, not a problem. Too bad Armory stopped it..." I trailed off just not wanting to think about the bitch.

"Armory?"

"The evil ex-wife from hell, and had a child with Michael...She hates me because I'm half my mom like I asked to be born, and get stuck at a dead-end job...."

"Wow...and she was the one supposedly dating Zackary, but I don't know why since she is an angel..." Said Nick.

It can explain how he was in the realm, and if so there is more problems than they realize. We walked to the ritual room, and it was past a hallway, up a flight of stairs, and we ended up at the library. Weird...the library was awesome since it was a big place with thousands of books on three floors and a winding staircase. A ton of comfortable chairs lined the place with people reading and leafing through books. It was heaven to me since I loved reading... I've been surrounded by so many dumb people at work that intelligence is refreshing...

We went to a bookcase, and then Nick pulled out a book. It shook and opened up into another secret room. Felix, Nick, and I went inside, and it led to a hallway filled with pictures of leaders and angels on the wall. We get to the end of the hall and stop at the door.

Nick went to the door and held up his hand. He glowed blue with his dragon power, and pointed it at the door. It shutters on the strength of the power, and it opened the room. He stepped inside and Felix and I trailed behind.

The ritual room is huge and all in blue with an angel mural on the ceiling. It's filled with everything one will need for a ritual. Swords. Herbs. Stones. All the items needed to do rituals. I still have my backpack on, and I took it off since there is a table to do the ritual on.

I get up to the table, and mom is near it in the corner.

"Good thing you made it, and I was worried when they said we had issues because of Zack and Austin. They are both fallen angels and can't be trusted." she told me. I knew already...

"Yes, I know I hope he died when I blasted him, and he fell off." I told her.

She laughed, "I hope so too since he was using you for Zack. He should have been dead a long time ago." My mom is just like me...That is awesome and I'm finally ready to take my place.

"She has me now, and I won't treat her the way Austin did. I'm not like the rest, which is why my ex wants me so bad. There is no one with my fierce protectiveness either." Felix said like I was his water in a very hot desert.

It made me happy to hear that. I'm finally able to get out of my job, and do something that matters. Everyone gave off strong, good emotions, and I loved it. I can get used to life here, move out, and then be happier. I can live with Felix and help find more AngelWitches. I'll quit Kyle's General Store, and turn in my last two weeks counting down the days, and thank god since it means no shitty schedule with very little coverage. No doing two departments or more at once with stupid demanding customers, and I can be happy...

Felix put the book in the middle of the table, and I took out the stuff to put on the table. Glitter. Ambrosia. Shirts. Candles and everything else I needed. Then finally the essence of Arch Angel. It's all there and time to finally come into my power then get out of retail.

"Don't forget the necklace I gave you." mom said. I pull it out and it glows with power.

"It recognizes you which is good since it means you are the leader, and you will lead your coven to battle. Your new goal is to find the rest of the Angel-Witch elements to complete the circle."

"Okay no problem I hope I can do it."

I pull it out and put it at the center. It glows once the power touches it.

"It recognizes you which is good since it means you will lead them to battle. Your new goal is to find the rest of the elements and complete the Angel-Witch circle."

"Okay, it's something I can do."

I pull out the candles and place them in the middle. The ambrosia is there followed by the wing glitter. I go ahead and put on the shirt to be ready for the wings. I put the arch angel essence in its spot. Everything is ready to go I hope.

"It has to be done by a powerful witch or

archangel leader. The ritual also binds an angel or Protector to their witch soulmate, and it gives the witch wings and the ability to heal very quickly. You won't age either. You will be a part of my coven since you are my daughter, and you can take over as the leader when I step down. The coven is called Wolf Water. Not only will you have the power over wolves, but water as well. Since you will be leader of your own coven it will give you power over all the elements as well. Felix will be the co leader and help you along the way. You also get to share his dragon, and Nick will be yours to help you in battle."

"You'll have me since I specially asked to be your Protector and Angelmate. It's also fate since I've been dreaming about you since I was little. I was made for you and we can work together to make everything good and prepare for what's coming." He said.

"Okay, I'm ready…" I told her to be ready to step into my power.

Mom sets up everything and five candles are on the table. Two candles stand for me and Felix.

"We are gathered here today to bring Angeline into her power as an AngelWitch. She is given the power of the Wolf Water Coven. She is inducted as an AngelWitch along with being bound to Felix which means his previous contracts are terminated."

The magic flowed in the room, and she took a lighter and lit the candles.

"I call the element water to the circle." She lit the

blue candle, and a dark blue circle appeared. It was a moving energy.

"I call fire to the circle..." She lit the red candle, and a red ring of moving fire surrounded us in a bubble.

"I call earth to the circle." She lit the green candle, and a green ring of energy surrounds us.

"I call air to the circle." A windy energy surrounded us as soon as she lit the yellow candle.

"Finally, it moves in all of us, and I call spirit to the circle." The last energy wave was a golden bubble enclosing us in a sacred space. I loved the feeling of the elements. The magic was really inviting like a warm blanket. Power rose up and encircled her like blue fire.

"My coven the Wolf Water Coven accepts you as one of their own, and now you have their powers running through your veins. Do you accept?"

I nodded and she directed the power toward me. It hits me and changes me completely. The shape materializes next to mom, and it's Michael.

"Sorry I'm late to the party. I had to evade a crazy ex. Here is my part. I accept you as an AngelWitch, and you have the power to fly, rapid healing, and Felix is your permanent Protector. I accept you as one of our own. Time to get your wings to fly."

He took his hands together, and hit me with his power. I fall to the ground and the energy bursts through me and something tingles and stretches. I finally got them. The power changes me into something I was meant to be, and I knew then that I'm finally home...

"Angeline I'm your Protector forever, and yours to keep and hold forever. I'll do anything to make you happy. I'll protect you with my last breath, and love you forever."

Felix picked me up, and kissed me. It makes power shoot through us, and I was in his head.... It bound us forever, and now I finally know what home felt like. I was meant to be with him. I kiss him back, and the world doesn't matter. I had come home. Home isn't a place, but instead it's a feeling where you belong. I'm happy. I finally have a person there all the time. It won't be perfect, but we will manage. Felix broke away and I feel empowered now. I'm stronger than I was, and it will be good to step into my new life.

The magic feels alive to me, and I can now feel everything more then I used to. My wings flex and I wonder how to fly.

"Now just a sprinkle of glitter, and ambrosia to allow you permanent access to the realm." Felix said handing me it.

Michael takes the essence of Archangel and hands me it.

"With the blessings of an archangel you are now one of us." I take it and I can finally see everything. It's official. I didn't even need to think about magic since I knew how to do it. The elements move and form into people.

The blue figure turns into a formless person, "I'm the water element spirit. My name is Aqua. I'll help you with the water element magic and when you find the water witch I'll empower her to make the coven strong with the power to call water creatures."

A red figure turned into a formless person beside Aqua.

"I'm Lavar the fire element. When you find the fire person I'll give you the powers of fire, and the ability to use fire magic."

A green figure formed into a person and then said, "I'm Leif the earth element. I will make you feel strong with the powers of earth by your side. A great power is coming, and you need all the witches by your side."

A yellow figure appeared too, and the last element besides spirit. "I'm Airey the air element. I'll bring the powers of air. The moment you have all of us the powers of the elements form the most powerful AngelWitches in Luxor. Just be careful since there are people willing to use that power for evil."

I smile, "I'll find them all, and we will defeat the powers before they destroy what's left of this world. I'll find them all."

The elements combined into one with a flash, and held their hands open. A stone was in the palm of her hands, and it was clear and glowing all the colors of the elements.

"This is the AngelWitch stone for the leader, and it will help you find them. All together it will create a magic so powerful it will destroy the evil threatening Luxor. Don't let Zack get his way, and always keep the stone with you." I take it and the stone fills me up with power.....

As soon as my skin touched the stone I was whisked away. I could feel all four of them in my head. Four girls with four different stories and backgrounds.

One girl in her room is looking for that one special guy to spend time with. One having an Obsession Spell on her because the guy who wanted her is a psycho. One witch running from an evil witch coven. One lost her way in the Crystal Crest realm after her twin ruined her life. I see it all and each of them has the power to help me stop the evil threatening this harmony I came back to myself.

Felix held me and said, "Are you okay?"

I smile, "Just fine at this point and I know how to find them and what they look like." Finding them is the easy part. The hard part will be convincing them to join us a long with their Angelmate."

"Yes, but it will be an adventure we will be doing together." He kissed me and my heart melted since I was excited. This move means more than me just becoming who I was. It also means that I now have someone who won't treat me like my ex did. I had a future now, and I could not be happier.

The ground shakes though and it feels like an earthquake is there. The elements and magic disappear and everything is chaotic. It's thrown into chaos, and people are running around I can feel people with my new powers.

I also felt a presence in the bodies like an ugly, evil person there. It's fighting with the good ones, and then I hit Zack…. Evil ex…unless I tried to get out I was screwed. It was supposed to be safe though. Then I felt another person too…Armory…I have no idea how she found out, but I don't like it one bit. I though my dad got rid of her but it didn't work.

I say fuck it and get mad. Felix was trying his best to hold me back, but I couldn't help it. I was hot on his heels. A force was dragging me to it against my free will. I had no control over it at all. I wanted blood and death. I go toward it all. And there they were Zack, ex, and Armory, and they were outside the force field.

"You are the girl we are looking for. My dad will be pleased when I deliver you to him. That was we won't have to worry about getting stopped by you."

Felix laughed, "I doubt you can take her since she is now a full AngelWitch. They are more powerful then you are all combined." He said sure of it all.

"Come on now no one can be more powerful than a full angel Michael should never have fallen for a witch in the first place. That way we would not even have to worry about another brat running around, and taking up more of Michaels money. Money I need to fund his other son." Armory said not caring she sounded like a selfish bitch.

Personally, I just wanted them to shut up and go away.

"Since you can't get past the force field you might as well just fuck off and die." I told them.

Armory gave us a wicked smile, "Actually someone on the inside already figured out a way to shut down the force field."

She has to be lying.... No one can figure it out. The once strong force field shuttered and flickered before it shut off completely like a light that turned off. Great just what we needed. The force field is down which means the island is no longer safe. She gave us an evil look. I resist the urge to be scared. I face them both ready to kick their ass. They charge us, and a smoke comes out making everything hard to see. It's not too long before someone grabs me, and I pass out....

.... I blacked out and felt like I was falling somewhere. My head rested on a pillow, and I slept again.

"Wake up..." A cruel voice told me. I open my eyes and find myself in a cell. A metal cell. I try to touch it and get shocked instead...Great. Just what I needed.

"That is one of the only metals that can contain an AngelWitch. Neat huh?" Zack said an evil glint in his eyes.

I glared at him wanting to rip him to shreds. I looked around the room and it was made of stone. A cave maybe? I don't know. It's going to look like a long day right now.

"Perfect to house my precious angel." My evil ex Austin said. I guess I didn't kill him like I thought I did.

"The next time I hit you I won't miss. Besides why are you both here? I'm now a full AngelWitch and that means you can't use me anymore...." I tell him wanting to reason with their crazy asses. Great...

"Well, now the ritual won't work obviously, but there are options since there are dark AngelWitches too..."

"Of course, for that ritual it will break the tie to your goody two shoes mate." Austin said as if it's the bad thing to happen to me,,,,

I need to find a way to get out. I want to keep Felix and not belong to evil Austin. I now need a way to contact Felix.

..Panic set in and I want to go now. I'd rather be at my job then here. I have no idea what to do.

"Oh, don't worry my brother is trying to find a way here to find you. I doubt he would. No one is allowed to Blood Mayne cave..." Zack sneered being an asshole to rub it in my face.

Being stuck here sucks. I really don't care for the damsel in distress bullshit or the panic because I'm stuck in a cage. It's the metal that keeps me here. My newly developed wings mock me since I can't fly my way out of here...yet. Without them I'd be screwed since it looks like a tall cave with a way out at the top. Even though I was not trained to fly I wanted to test it out anyway.

I get off the ground and let it unfurl. They are pure white, and I flex one of the wings. They are soft to the touch. I try to move them and the gently flap... that's it since I don't know how to fly...I hate being in a cell and it definitely looks like a prison one.

Behind bars too...A cot, sink, toilet, and the basics. No television since it looks like a cave. The red granite walls and hard stone floors are not exactly inviting. It smells like mildew like an old person lived here, but all caves smell like it.

Zack and Austin stood there arms crossed watching me like psychos. Sure, stare at the newly changed AngelWitch. I told my wings and stared back at them. The door opens and Armory comes through the door. Bitch. If I could kill her I would.

She looks as perfect as ever wearing a black shirt and jeans. She wore boots, and had perfectly done make up.

She gave me a nasty smile, "Freaks like you should not exist I don't know why my ex fell for you whore of a mom...But at least he pays me enough to not need a job cause I had his child. I still don't know what to do with the little bastard he is just like your dad too. It sickens me. But no issue. The moment you turn into Austin's toy I'll make you kill your mom which will end the annoying witch and angel truce. Then a war will break out..."

I hate this place even more then my shitty retail job. I love rage too. I let it flow through me, and it made my power glow. I knew instinctively. I know exactly how to tap into it. Rage is my best friend. I love it, and the magic is like a long-lost best friend. I knew exactly how to access it. I throw it at the bars, and it doesn't do shit.... I really wished I could talk to Felix at this point. I hope he is okay, and that he is coming to get me back. The stuff that kept me in check may burn me, but I can still find a way to get out. I can contact Felix with my mind since we are tied together now. He is my Angel soulmate after all. I sit down on the floor and close my eyes. I think about his face and the way he makes me feel....

A voice that sounded far away answered, "Can...you...hear...me."

I concentrate harder and follow the voice.

"Can you hear me? It's Felix..."

"Yes, I can." I replied back.

Laughter on the other end, "Good. I knew you would be there. I'm trying to find you, and I'm in the realm. Your dad is with me and mom is on the dragon. Once you were taken we scoured the realm, and I found out that I can tune into your energy."

Thank god, help is on the way....

"I knew you would come for me." I told him.

"Okay, and I can feel you in the building we are in so stay put for me." He told me.

"Roger that I was trying to break out anyway, and failing at it..." I told him.

"That's my girl. I love you and if anything happened to you I wouldn't know what to do with myself..." Awww....my heart melted at that since I feel the same way.

"They are trying to break the bond between us to turn me dark...I don't want to belong to my ex. I want to belong to you..." I don't want them to cut the tie between me and Felix, and it worries me.

"You will still be mine. A soulmate bond can't be broken anyway. Anyone even trying to break the bond will be destroyed." He said reassuring me nothing can happen to it.

"Okay, hurry up I don't want to stay here for too long..." I said not wanting to be there anymore, but I have to.

I open my eyes and get up off the floor. Felix was coming for me. I was sure of it.

Armory, Zack, and Austin were just sitting there pacing.... I really hate Austin, so I let him have it.

"So, you can't have me and never treated me right, but now you want me permanently tied to you?" I asked him wondering how bonkers he is....

"You know we are meant to be together. I never wanted that bitch in the first place. I only wanted to get closer to you..." He lied.

"Yeah right. You ignored me when we were dating, Didn't talk to me. You were supposed to be someone I can depend on, but you turned into an asshole." I said.

"You weren't supposed to break up with me at all. I'm your soulmate not the other guy. But soon we won't need to worry about it." he told me like a psycho.

I just laughed to myself. Felix will find me then I won't be alone.

"I don't think it was about love at all. You don't stalk the people you love." I told him.

Austin stared at me. I don't think he even knows what love is just possession. How I'm all knowing when I'm trapped I don't know. I definitely get to be free at last. I was tired at this point. Between the ceremony and everything else I was ready to say fuck it and rest on the makeshift bed...I knew I would not have to wait long for Felix since he is my Protector after all. I feel good knowing he is coming for me. He will find me then get me out before I become someone else's.....

.... A crash got the people holding me captives attention. Zack and Austin ran to see what it was about. That left me with only Armory to deal with....

"That had better not be those damn dogs barking at nothing again, Hellhounds suck as pets, but are good for guarding at times...." She told me.

I'm just sitting in the cage in shock not knowing what to do. One of the dogs dart in front of the cage and appear like magic. He was just standing there in front guarding me. I just hope Felix is safe and that he knows how to stop them. Armory just stood there babysitting me and all I could think of was I hope I get out of this thing before I starve, go to the bathroom or cramp...I hate being stuck like this...I would never wish this on my worst enemy. I checked to see how far Felix was away...I closed my eyes and sat down searching for his energy, and he was pretty close like outside the door close. I was happy since I did not want to be here for long.

Armory was just sitting there with the dog thing...A bored expression on her face. I hoped Felix knew how to defeat a thing like this because I did not see a way out of it. I hoped he knew how to defeat one. The damn thing started barking and Armory sprang into action. Her eyes turned pure black, and she had fangs. So much for being an angel. That and her wings are black not white which meant she was not a good angel to begin with.

The door shook to the place, and then it disintegrated....

Interesting...

Felix was behind it and Michael was right beside him.

Felix saw me and smiled, "Thank god you are fine."

Armory looked at Michael and glared, "Really Michael you are going to do this to me? Betray me?" She said.

"You captured my daughter, and drugged your son to the point where he didn't even recognize himself..." Michael said.

She crossed her arms and glared, "Well, it was for

his own good since you couldn't handle the little brat. Neither could I. He was just a paycheck after all that's it. Not a person to me. You chose all my friends over me, and I had to find a way to get you back. Your mind games just made me that pissed off, and I wanted the government to pay me money. Hence why I eat your paycheck each day." She said he meant nothing to him.

"Well, you never cared about my son in the first place since you never let me see him, and took full custody of him from me. You locked him up three times just to control him, and then wondered why he hates you. Hell, he is so drugged up it's affecting his powers, and I wish you were dead." Michael told her.

"Well, the little brat needs to be controlled since I don't know what to do anymore.... He was just another paycheck after all." she replied making me wish he would just kill her already...She is a heartless cunt that deserves to die.....

"Well, then you are dead to me. And time to be done with you once and for all. You have committed treason since you tried to take my daughter away from me. First you take away my son, and then try for my daughter.... No, I'll take care of our son, and your dog means nothing to me since it's an illusion."

Michael muttered something in a weird language and then the thing vanished leaving only Armory....

"Thanks for nothing I guess I'll have to kill you myself."

Michael laughed at her threat. Armory charged at him, but she just looked sad as if he caught her. He grabbed her by the neck and gave it a twist.... She got thrown on the floor like a useless rag doll. Dead. I smiled at that since she deserved it, I hated her anyway.

"Well, issue solved since our son will be raised by me. I'll show him how to use his powers, and how to be a man finally. He will go to school, and act like a normal boy finally. All she taught him is criticism, fear, and just drugged him to control him."

Felix smiled, "Told you she was trouble. I saw it coming from a mile away, and all she wanted a paycheck for was to buy things for her, and not her son."

I agreed since I don't want to call her mom at all. Michael broke the bars, and I was finally free to go. I stepped out of the cell, and I was happy to finally be free of that place, I fell into Felix's arms, and he held me close to him,

"I killed Austin for you and as for Zack he will be placed in prison where he belongs. You don't have to worry about seeing him ever again." he told me happily.

"Good, and you are so much better than the rest of the guy's I've dated." I told him.

"I'm better than them since I'm yours forever...." he told me.

"Yes, and we can find the rest of the girls to complete the circle." I told him.

"Yes..." And then we all got out of the hell dimension. We rode the dragon back to the castle. I was happy at that point since I loved being there instead of that place. I was right where I belonged....

Back at Michael's palace we all had dinner together. I was next to my Angelmate and Protector. Even Kalisa is there, and smiling....

"Next is my 2 weeks at Kyle's and then we search for the witches. It's not easy since they will come from all walks of life, and come with their Angelmate. I do have a device that can find them so it's not an issue. We have to find them to form the most powerful coven out there." I told them,

"Yes, and you do have the angels to help you in this place, and your dragon Nick too." Felix said.

Michael smiled, "I'll have my hands full in undoing the damage Armory caused to everything. Your Brother Raiden will be a strong fighter, and even captain of the guard." Dad said.

I'll call him dad since he is one of the best dads out there. He took his son away from his pathetic waste of a mom, and he cares about him enough as a person. He doesn't use him as a paycheck like the mom did. Armory was being paid money to help afford him. She had Raiden to get back at him for choosing other women over him. I hate women like her, and I'm happy she is dead.

Austin is dead which means I no longer have to

worry about him stalking me. I can fly now, and finally learn how to use my gifts.

"Yes, and now let's have fun the last two weeks at Kyle's" Kalisa said with a glint in her eye.

"Yep, we will...." I told her and we all toasted to that....

CHAPTER NINETEEN

Angeline's last two weeks.....

Felix and I are moving all my stuff to the Angelic realm since we are staying with Michael now. I went in personnel in the back of Kyle's. I went to personnel and told them I'm moving away, and that is why I 'm quitting. I was happy to do that, and I can't wait to stop working for a company that doesn't care.

I drove myself since I did not want to seem suspicious in this realm, or draw too many heads. I've changed since I had to turn into an AngelWitch and I'm the one that can control all the elements. With all four girls I can stop the evil and form a powerful coven of witches. I still needed to find them, and it will take time. I have decided to go to school in the Angelic realm instead and thankfully they have it online. I'm happy about that since I can study while looking for the girls.

I needed to finish my last two weeks to look good

in the eyes of the company. I wanted to go back to a different retail stores like Nightwatch or even the Angel Emporium. That might be awesome to try in order to see how different it can be. There are times when I don't hate retail like some of the people there pick me up when I've had a bad day. There are good times and bad times working there. Sometimes I didn't mind working there, and times when I'd rather shove a chainsaw up my ass then work there.

I have Monday and Tuesday off from Kyle's so that means I can visit my friendly neighborhood witch Ginger to tell her about the events.

I head for her shop and as usual the idiots on the road this time can't drive. I park in a spot, and go inside her shop. The smell of incense hits me, and it calms me down. A bell rang above me to let her know someone was in the shop. Lavender is always calming to me, and it makes my day brighter. With my witch powers her shop felt more alive with magic. The energy of the room has a feel on its own. It might be awesome to work here too since it would be fun to help people in a magical way.

I can totally get used to it...

Ginger was currently helping someone, so I waited patiently. I looked around. I know the uses for most of this stuff since I've been training on my witch side with my mom. Love, money, beauty, and I can now shield myself to people. It's awesome since they are not interfering with my brain anymore. I'll love a job that will allow me to put my skills to use.

Ginger wore a long, black dress that looked like a second skin on her. She is stunning too, and I can't wait to tell her everything. I would come here on my breaks at Kyle's since it's along the way. I have known her for a very long time, and she can teach me a thing or two about my witch side, and help me with the girls.

I looked over at her, and she was finishing with the person.

"Call me if this doesn't work so we can go over other options too.." she said.

The person left and she met my eyes.

"Hey, how is everything?" She asked.

"I'm an AngelWitch now, and Felix is mine for good. Zack is stopped for now, and I'm in charge of getting a coven together of others like me. I've turned in my last two weeks because I no longer need the job since I have another."

Her eyes widen, "I'm glad since I know it's easier on you knowing who you are now. You are going to love being a witch and if you want to help me around my shop you can."

"Thanks, I will help around sometime since it's more interesting then working at Kyle's.." I tell her excited now.

"Yep. Yep, and you will get to use magic for people versus serving idiots and folding clothes. Picking out spells for people is very satisfying to me." She said. She actually loves it, and I'll love it too it might actually be fun.

"I've already turned in my last two weeks." I told her.

"That is good. I know how much you hated going there, and their emotional states are hard to deal with too. Once you came into my shop dirtier than usual with their energy." She said.

I shivered, "That day it took longer than usual to get all the junk off me..."

"Well, at least you will be done with it soon," she told me.

I was grateful it was almost done. I can't stand Penny either since she is a shitty manager. I was done with being treated like shit there, and Megan was a pain since she punished me twice for a mistake I made. I mean come on it was an accident. I didn't deliberately break the watch...I'm tired of being worked to the bone for a company that doesn't care. Sometimes doing phones, fitting room, shoes, jewelry, and accessories is a pain in the ass. It's a pain when I have to watch them all at once. Then if you do one job right you get yelled at for doing another. I was watching the phones and fitting room but got yelled at for writing work stuff and not zoning shoes since I hate it...I don't like being in charge of multiple things since we are so short staffed. Then don't get me started on the bullshit favoritism. This cunt tried to accuse me of sleeping with her ex, and it wasn't even true. She ignores me one day, and the next she gossips about me to her coworker saying I bet you she won't even admit to it. Come on...I hate her ass. I can't wait to leave her behind. I have to act like I like her even though I hate her and hope she dies. Everyone around me hates her too. She just walks around doing nothing, and she acts like she owns the place. I dread seeing her but at least I don't have to deal with her for very long.

"Yep. I'll be done with retail and free. I have to go, and do some research on the girls more since I need to find them ASAP. I'll see you later," I told her.

"See you later then, and whenever you want a job just let me know." She told me.

"I will," then I gave her a hug and left.

I went back to my apartment. It's the same till my last day at work. Then I'll move, and I already have a laptop to do research. I don't even know if the girls know if they are AngelWitches which is a problem in itself. I also have to find their angels. They are their Protectors too. I know they give off energy so we just have to hone into them. I also need to stop off at the island since they will have more information on them. After the shield collapsed they built a better one that can't be tampered with at all. I was taken because someone from the inside tampered with it, and this time they made it tamper proof. One that will let in only certain people. I like it since it will definitely make sure the creature is allowed to be there and keep out the people wanting to harm us. I headed to the apartment, and Felix is already there since his car is parked in front. He uses a car in this area, and it's a red sports car since he loves going fast.

He used to be a street drag racer, but that was a part of his past. Not to mention he doesn't want to seem like he appeared out of thin air, and he needs to appear normal to people. I parked my car next to his, and unbuckled my seat belt. I get the key out, and unlock the door to the apartment. It still has some items in there. Some are in boxes, and especially the memories Austin left behind. I don't want to remember him, and I'm happy he is finally gone. Just the important stuff is out. The stuff I use the most, and my clothes are still in my closet. I might as well keep my old uniform and name tag to remind me where I don't want to go. Once I'm done with retail I'm out.

After my life was in danger, and I was about to lose Felix I realized just how much he truly meant to me. He means the world to me, and he is staying with me at all times. I never want him to leave my side. Nearly losing him made me never want to change it at all. It's not just my life it's his too since we are connected.

Felix sat on the black leather couch with his laptop on his lap. He looked sexy doing it. Probably surfing the web or taking care of Protector stuff, he is the leader after all.

"How was talking to Ginger?" He asked me and then looked up at me giving me a sexy smile.

I smile back at him, "Not bad I just updated her on the stuff that went down."

"Good. I'm keeping an eye on Zack's cell since he

was placed there, and it looks like he is just sitting there. It might not hold forever since he might be involved with a darker thing, and it's why we need the girls...Don't expect this to be easy, and there are more people trying to find the girls to kill them before they form with us...." He said, and he was right...

My eyes widen still, "Well, I knew there is evil coming, but not that you had access to Zack's cell..."

He looked at me like he thinks I've lost it, "I do since I'm head of the Protectors, and he is in a holding cell. I help make sure the witches and their mates stay safe. I also keep track of them to look out for their Angelmate, and it might not be easy as it is with us either. We lucked out. Some fight it and others don't...some can be in love with a person and their Angel too. Nick is going to help since he can see energy. He helped me find you and watched you from a far..." He said.

Aww.... He was stalking me even before we officially met how cute.

"Yes, and we can follow wherever with our wings unless it's in the Crystal Crest realm."

"Yes." He said. I loved flying and the more I practiced the better I got. I needed to leave retail for good. I'll have fun my last two weeks in using my powers on the mean customers. the bitchy manager and coworker." I said.

The thought made me grin...Getting the bitch back will be fun. I hate her so it will be fun to do that...The bitchy coworker Alice Johnson. I could kill her even if she is tall and joining the Crystal Crest elites. Yes, you fight for this realm, but it doesn't mean you can walk all over people. She definitely needs to be taught a lesson. I was glad since they all but fucked over Jasmine in her promotion. They also promoted the wrong supervisor.

They promoted a rude bitch, and she dropped the ball since she lost a customer's ring order and didn't get fired for it. I hate it and bullshit like this is why I'm leaving retail. I'll leave it far behind and dedicate my time to finding the girls since I'll be their leader after all. I really needed a change since I can't move up or change my area in Kyle's. I'd die before I become a supervisor. Nope. After all the years I worked there it's time to move on to bigger and better things. All the regulars, people I've met, and situations I've been in.

I went to Felix and put my arms around his neck, and he put his arms around me in turn. I feel safe in his arms. He is my other half. My life, and I don't mind it at all since he is the best in the world. I love him and I would not have it any other way. He kissed me and the world went away. I can connect with him on every level. I don't know where I began and his ended.

Mine…All mine and that is the best part of this journey. I'm never alone. He deepened the kiss, and soon relieved me of all the stress I was feeling.

Afterward, we planned a trip to the island. I really need to contact Nick to start the search for the first girl. All of the elements AngelWitches are essential to forming the circle. The first one we need to look for is fire. She will be fun to find first. Felix and I headed to the car to make our way to the island. But to get there we need to go to Luxor. I needed to get something from mom and fill her in on the events. I'll tell her about my turning in my two weeks and finding the girls. The drive was quiet with Felix concentrating on the road. I'm just off in la la land fantasizing about my last two weeks.

We pass the Crystal Crest realm and when we hit Luxor I can feel it. The magic is welcoming here, and I can feel the energy start to calm me. I was already calm, but now I'm already at peace with everything. I love it since we are in the streets now with creatures driving places. Some actually fly around too. Even the fake sun was out and shiny. Vampires can come in this one since it's not a danger to them. I love it here, and Felix easily navigated the streets. Ten minutes later he stopped the car, and we got out. We get to the gate, and it opens slowly. We go in, and walk to the door of her mansion.

I knocked and it opened. Mom was standing in the living room area, and she smiled, "I'm happy to see you safe and sound. I heard about Zack and Austin and what they did. Too bad Armory had to die, but she had it coming with the way she treated Michael. She was horrible, and kept Michael from seeing Raiden unless they were in person. She didn't need to know about your dad, and I till we were married. You see she is so horrible that she doesn't want anyone around her son. She always wanted control and custody of him since she wanted your dad miserable because he doesn't care about her like he used to. She has been such a bitch to women he has dated in the past by forcing him to choose the girl and his son. It killed Michael since Armory used him for money for child support. She used it on herself and not her child. She deserved to die, and when Raiden went away she was happy since he was a burden to her." Mom said. I just shook my head since she was just as bad as Felix's ex...

"And now that dad is free he can raise his son the way he wants to and no one will miss her, and I'm glad she is dead too since it means I won't have to deal with her. She means nothing to me, and I'll never call her anything." I told him.

"Well, I'm glad Zack is in prison since it means he can't hurt you, and Austin deserved what he got since he was a stalker," she said.

I agree with her, and then it's time to leave. I need to go in order to find the girls.

"I'll catch up with you some other time, and let you know about what happens. I have to go back to the island to find the girls and start the search."

She smiled, "Take care of my daughter Felix and stay out of trouble."

He smiled, "I will and I'm happy to be with your daughter instead of my evil ex trying to get my money."

"Yes. And I'm happy my daughter has someone treating her right. Austin ruins everything. Find the girls and go on."

After a hug and a kiss on her cheek Felix and I make our way to the realm.

We go outside to the car, and head to the secret part to get to the Angelic realm. After a good 20 minutes we make it there. And Felix parks the car at a spot that is used to house cars to make it to the realm. We get out and head to the force field. The moment I get there I can feel the energy of the place. I know I'm home. My home was finally welcoming to me, and once I lived here it will be good to finally call a place home. I've never felt that before since my parents are out of the picture after my foster parents kicked me out at 18. They were more into drugs then me. I never had a good relationship with my adopted parents. It's beautiful here and instead of driving I fly. I know another way to get to the island and it's more hidden too. You have to match the energy signature they have or else it will kill you.

I unfurl my wings, and I make them appear from a white feather tattoo on my back to a real-life wing. One flex and that is their cue to come to life. I flex them and it wants to flex a muscle that has been curled up way too long. It was freeing not having to worry about cars and traffic. Even the people in Luxor can't drive. It's not something I enjoy either since I have road rage. I run and flap my wings, and take to the sky.

Felix is there leading the way, and I follow him since he knows the way better than I do. As the leader of the Protectors, he is in their offices taking care of the people under him. The wind hits me as I fly, and it's calming to me. Freeing too since I can go wherever I want no car needed.

Angels fly past like they are at ease, and it's something natural for them since they were born like that. After following Felix for some time there is a familiar shape next to us. Nick the dragon we met on the island.

"Follow him since he will show you how to get in." Felix said.

After a good 20 minutes we see a cave ahead. Nick lands on the ground in front of the door, and transforms back into a regular human. I land on my feet, and the wings turn back into tattoos. Then Felix lands next to me.

"This is the new way to get in since it was obvious that it was there. This way is more secret, and less people know about it too. The forcefield alone wasn't enough. Now it's in a cave only the people closest to us know about. We have to have a safe place for the girls and for our leaders." He said, and then he went up to the door. Nick placed his finger on a pad and types in a code.

"Welcome Nicholas you may enter," a robotic voice said. I wondered how it was recorded, but it was done by a machine.

"All you have to do is type in the code 1025, and

put your finger on the scanner since it will work for both of you." He said informing me.

I scanned my finger and inputted the code.

"Welcome Angeline you may enter."

Then I went through the door, and Felix followed behind me.

Finally...home. It hasn't changed one bit. The door led to the complex and the island. Instead of seeing dad we went straight to the island first. The complex is still the same, and we needed to make our way to the main area. All the angels we passed were saying hi, and asking how I was doing. Zack can't interfere anymore, and I was just happy to not be in any danger. In order to look for the girls we needed to find their energy signatures. Every potential Angel-Witch is kept track of since they are that rare. That is how they found me since it was Ginger who alerted them to my presence. She was sent to watch over me along with Kalisa. We also need to find their Angel-mate since they can't come into their power without them.

"Since you all have been gone we have been on the lookout for the girls. So far we believe they are spread over both realms. One of them is a fire Angel-Witch, and she is someone very special since she has a book that we need to use in order to perform the ritual to come as a coven. She is unknown name wise, but there are other convers searching for her. It's a good witch versus evil witch coven and they will get mad on both sides if we get involved." He said and I could tell he is not too happy about the other convers.

Great, just what we need a war. We get to the main room, and the main console. Nick hits a button, and then all the potential Angel Witches pop up.

"The ones we are looking for are colored a different way. All the potentials are white but the ones we need are the colors of their elements." Then he hit another button. Only four of them stick out. The girls we need.

"What about their protectors?" I asked wondering if they need to keep them safe.

"They are keeping an eye on them already. A Protector already knows who his mate is, and then they find them to watch over them to make sure they are not harmed." Nick said.

"I knew about you Angel before I even became the head of the Protectors. I was in a bad place at the time after my ex left me for someone, and then demanded money after she knew I got a high paying job. Then I knew just what to do after getting too drunk. I saw the people hiring for the head of Protectors. They are chosen sometimes, and sometimes they put up a flier. The other catch is you have to ask them about finding the girl in your dreams, and that is how you know you are one. That is why you are mine, and I'm yours. The Angels in charge knew I was one, and that is when I would find my dark-haired angel one day while you were working the counter...I followed your colored energy signature to your job, and then there was a trace of Ginger's magic signature, and that is how we found each other." He told me.

It made my heartbeat fast knowing he was mine and that I was his Angel. I don't mind the nickname now.

"Yes, and the angels and dragons also work together as well since they are stronger together. The dragons can defeat the demons trying to hurt their AngelWitches." Nick said.

I was in charge of all this, yet it was hard to believe.

"So which one is the first one we need to find?" I asked.

Nick stepped up to the screen, and pointed to a red one.

"She is the fire witch we need, and in the most danger. And in the Luxor realm along with the water one. The earth one is in Crystal Crest along with the air one," he said.

"Yes, I agree we need to make finding her the top priority. The question is how and where is she?" I asked.

"She will take more time to get intel on. Even her angel is nowhere to be found. I suggest you get retail out of the way to find time. Either way it won't be easy..." he said.

I believed it. The blip can be anywhere in Luxor. It will be hard to search for her if she doesn't want to be found. She does need to be found since she has the book we need. We would have to have a map closer to her location, and I'm sure it's the girl we are looking for.

"It won't be easy period since we aren't the only ones after her, and once they find out then they might try to kill her for it. Her Angelmate will keep her safe. I hope," Nick said sighing.

Yes, and I hope so too since they are supposed to protect them.

"Is there a way to tell if one is near?" I asked Nick.

"Yes, We created the device to detect their energy to make tracking them easier."

Then he stepped away, and he was away for a few minutes, and came back with something in his hands. He was holding a box. A black box, and he opened it standing on a red pillow was a bracelet.

"It can also detect when their Angelmate is near since they are the color of the witch they are bonded to." He picked up the device, and I went forward. I lifted my left hand, and he put the device on me.

Once it touched my skin it came to life, and it showed a map with little dots.

"It's a map of the area, and it will show the Angel-Witches location of the area they are in. Not exact, so you will have to get closer so it can show up." Nick told me. I just nod it fits perfectly on me too. This device will come in handy.

"I'll also help you guys too since the dragon shifters find this important too."

It's not just about the girls but about everyone.

I have a few weeks till I'm out of retail for good. I can even go home and cuddle with Felix it's a good few days off. Then Hell for 4 days off two and work last four. I smile at myself since I'll be done with hell soon. I have an awesome device to use, and it will be a good challenge. Even though I have the device I still need to pinpoint exactly where she is... That will be the hard part for sure especially if someone is trying to get her. I need to find her name. I will though and they can stay with me in Michael's place or here where they belong. I look at the Bracelet...interesting. Felix stepped toward me to glance at it. Now we just have to have a starting point.

"Neat. And now we can find her easily as long as we are in the area." Felix said. I just wondered if people are going to be looking for her too, and it's not going to be easy. I'll have time after retail has ended. It will end soon. Then I can move on to something more important than picking up after idiots and answering their dumb questions. I'm also sick of being treated like shit by people who can't even shop for themselves. Kyle is irritating as fuck, and Megan needs to go away. I thought of all this, but I really need to get back to reality.

Felix looked at me, "Are you okay?"

I nod, "Fine just have to get through the next two weeks before retail destroys what little I have left. It's not easy dealing with it all."

It's not easy since all I had to worry about was

getting through retail and dodging Austin. Now it's different. At least retail will go away for good, and I'll be better off without it. Retail sucks on a day-to-day basis. Just the thought of going to Kyle's is enough to make me sick. The people working there are idiots, and one tried to get me fired over his stupid watch breaking on me. He just had to get me to adjust it instead of letting a professional do it. Then the fucker had the balls to take it to someone else while she was watching the counter. She didn't even work there, and the fucker had the nerve to tell the manager too. Fuck this place. And don't even get me started on dealing with the customer service people some of them. I especially hate the asshole Travis since he called a manager because I didn't want to go on register since I had to relieve my friend for break. They act like they own us, and there are like three of them that won't fight me on the keys. Since I'm one of three jewelry people I hope they find someone else to replace me.

It's a long process when I'm there. The customers treat you like you are stupid. I'm sick of it and I'll be happy when I'm done with it. Just need to get through the weekends. I'll finally be done. I sigh and sit down at a nearby chair. It's comfortable. I stretch out and feel the muscles straining. Tension went away. I was ready.

I saw Ginger, mom, and discussed with Nick plans for the girls. By 2:00 I was starving so we went to the cafe there. I got my food and Felix, and I sat down at a table. I was so hungry I practically devoured it. I was happy to still be able to eat. Food is better than anything else.

I had a good lunch there since they have burgers, fries, and my favorite energy drink. I love their stuff since it's always good. They have a good place there, and it even has chairs, tables, and couches. Plenty of comfortable chairs to relax while people are in their offices or wherever. There is even a few flat screen televisions too, and it shows news from Luxor, Crystal Crest, and the Angelic realm. I love it all. I looked over at the one for Luxor. Queen Diana is the head of the realm, and she is trying to make things easier with laws on creature rights. Vampires and werewolves exist. I'll also have to be up to date on the history of the realm. Especially since my mom comes from there.

It's going to be different being a leader. I wasn't even a supervisor at my job now I'm a leader. I can learn how to use magic to fight back, and I'm sure Felix will help me learn moves from him.

"Are you okay?" Felix asked me.

I nod, "Just thinking about all the stuff I have to do."

"You'll get it, and I was born for it so I can help you with everything." he said.

I was happy to not be alone in this. I ate my food. It filled me up and got me ready for the rest of the day. The energy drink helps keep me going at times like these. I needed to start soon. Not only is the girl somewhere hiding but so is her Angel. At least she is safe I hope...

I look around the room, and there are Angels all over the place, and dragons too. Some stare at me since I'm sure they know who I am now. Everyone is talking to each other and enjoying their company. The only thing missing is someone to guide them. I've never been a leader, but I has Felix who has, and it will work out I hope. The evil will be stopped with the coven together.

The television screen has news on it, and nothing new happening at all. Just fights going on in Crystal Crest which was always about a policy or two. Murders here and there. It's different for Luxor too just watching the news since there are laws for vampires, werewolves, and other creatures.

"What rules are there in the Angelic realm?" I asked Felix.

"No one is allowed here unless they are an Angel or angelic being. You can't date a human since they can die over time. Angels and witches dating is allowed since a witch has powers a human doesn't. No killing humans either unless they try to kill you. No stealing. There is no need to steal anyway since I will willingly give you my heart." Felix said. Then he kissed me, and the world flew away. It was so good to be with him. I finally know what a healthy relationship is like. I was on Cloud 9, and he deepened the kiss. It felt good to be with him. The magic between us connected us mind to mind. He is unlike any guy

I've felt before. I love him, and I'm glad he is permanently mine. I want a future with him. Austin never treated me like a person. I was a pet someone to leave and use in the gutter. He pulled away leaving me breathless. I loved feeling like that he made things worth it in the end.

I love it, and I pull back.

Nick cleared his throat. He is breathless like he runs.

"You might want to come with me for a minute. Angel and Felix something happened..." he said. I got up and put away my trash. Then I followed him, and Felix was right behind me. After a few short cuts it was right back to the control room.

"And what is it?" I asked him.

Nick sighed, "Apparently the girl's angel is here, and he lost the fire witch."

It was my turn to sigh since that is a huge problem. It also meant we need to find her, and keep her safe before something bad happens to her.

"Awesome. Just bring the angel into the room." I told him.

Nick walks out of the room, and a few minutes later an angel comes in. They lost their witch and it was our job to find them... To be continued in Ember's Gift!

ACKNOWLEDGMENTS

I would like to thank my amazing editor Alethea Garcia for making it better then the last. Thank my family, friends and my amazing supportive boyfriend. This book is in its second version and I can't wait till the rest are redone! I plan on publishing more books and can't wait to see where it takes me!

ABOUT THE AUTHOR

Jessica Samuels is an author who writes paranormal romance, horror and thrillers and she loves to stream, read, cook and play games!

This is where to find the AngelWitch series if you want to read the old stories before it is rewritten. It needs major changes so it will be revamped so if you want to see it before then join my paid Substack newsletter, become a Ko-fi member, Patreon member, or join my website's paid tier and you can see it all!

Subscribe to my Substack for all news!

https://authorjessicasamuels.substack.com/

Website: https://jessicasamuelsauthor.wordpress.com/

Patreon: https://patreon.com/jdsamuels25

Ko-fi: https://ko-fi.com/jdsamuels

Discord for readers! https://discord.gg/Mus8xwQjR5

Author channel link: https://www.youtube.com/c/JessWolfie

Gaming channel: https://www.youtube.com/channel/UCwO5Why2tii4WA3yqEksclw

Twitch: https://www.twitch.tv/wolfiewitchcat25

Bluesky: https://bsky.app/profile/jesswolfie.bsky.social

Threads: https://www.threads.net/@jesswolfieswonderfulworld

Buy Me A Coffee! https://www.buymeacoffee.com/jdsamuels21

Links to everything: https://authorjess.carrd.co/

ALSO BY JESSICA SAMUELS

Ghost Reaper

Book 1:

Layla FireStar is an insurance rep by day, and a ghost reaper by night. Her passion is setting free the ghosts who have been trapped by the evils of the world. However, she has to be able to survive her life on earth.

While working her day job Layla will be summoned by an unlikely source who will teach her things she never knew. She will learn who she is and where she comes from. She will set Theodosius and Alister free from their torment, and show them love.

Love brought them together, but will love tear them apart? Will Layla be able to survive without her shifter mate Silas, and join forces and hearts with Theodosius and Alister? Or will she falter and be on her own?

Come follow us on this journey of love, loss, sex, passion, and freedom. Enjoy the passion of these interactions as they all reap the rewards of ghost reaping.

18+/Mature Audience due to content that may not be suitable for all readers.

Ghost Possession

Harley Calix is a demon anthologist in the realm of Luxor. She's madly in love with her boyfriend Roman, who's a vampire. They live their days in Cain's Palace left to them by Layla Firestar, who's the ghost reaper.

Harley and Roman are contacted by Daemon for a job to find his roommate and best friend DeMarcus. Everything changes in less than twenty-four hours. Possession, finding a new realm, and fighting against the evilest creatures they'd ever seen.

Everything shifts when the panty dropping Noah Jones isn't who he says he is. Will they be able to untangle the multiple spirits that have been spell bound together to create these demons, or will they get caught up in the extracurricular activities and become demons themselves?

Spicy book!

Supernatural Agency

Part 1 Supernatural Agency

Layla Firestar starts an agency that fights the supernatural beings that threaten her existence. When she comes upon a demonic creature that isn't from her world she has to make a choice. If she consumes him then she will upset the balance of good and evil, but if she allows him to continue he will end her.

She doesn't allow anything harm her family in anyway, but it could be her downfall when she comes into a new form of existence. She has to learn how to maintain and train herself to transform into her new form when it's needed or else she will end worlds.

Knowing she needs help she recruits Harley Calix to help her and meets a new powerful being. Introduced to her by the leader of the Death Realm Salina Sinclare proves herself a valuable member of the team.

Part 2 Killer Contract Agency

Salina Sinclare was born and raised in Crystal Crest, but gains her power from a family heirloom. It looks like a fashionable piece of jewelry, but it possesses the ability to do so much more. When she's recruited from the Death Realm to run her family's legacy known as the Killer Contract Agency she proves her power is valuable.

When she goes on her first case she runs into Darrel Crichton who's the evilest demon in the Angel Witch Utopia Realm. He's contracted by a leader possessed by another demon to end Layla and Harley's existence. Salina, however, runs into her rival from a past life and shows her strength with the flick of her wrist.

Part 3 Demon Agency

Harley Calix continues her demon anthology and runs the Demon Agency for Layla Firestar. When she gets the shock of a lifetime she transforms into something bigger than she ever thought possible. She learns that her heritage is connected in more ways than one to Layla Firestar.

Finding out that she herself has the grace of an angel proves that she can shift into her new form and then back into her human form with ease. The glow she cast off is enchanting and invites her enemies in only to disintegrate them with the same power. She learns exactly who and what she is by simply reading and listening.

Follow these three as they find their way into a new way of life and family.

One spicy scene the rest is about revenge they are back!

Made in the USA
Coppell, TX
30 April 2025